I0734277

GROWN ASS MEN

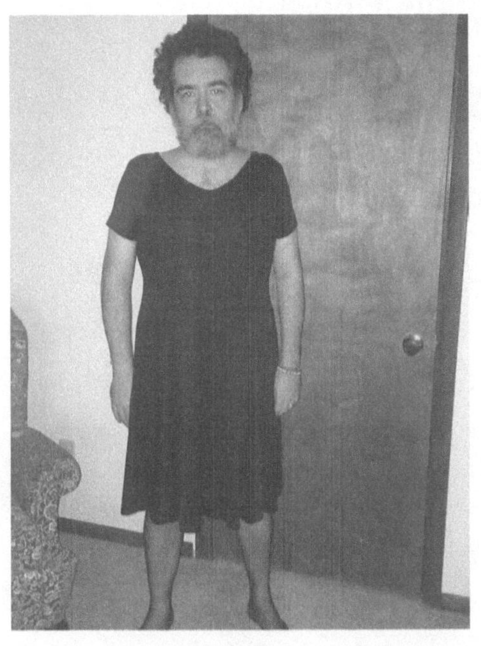

stories by

Daniel Crocker

Luchador Press

Big Tuna, TX

Copyright © Daniel Crocker, 2020

First Edition 1 3 5 7 9 10 8 6 4 2

ISBN: 978-1-952411-06-9

LCCN: 2020935483

All photos: Margaret Crocker

Acknowledgments:

Some of these stories have appeared in: *Drunk Monkeys, New World Writing, The Coil* (Where "This Love Story Has a Zombie in It" was a Luminaire finalist for best prose in 2014) and *The Brown Bottle*.

Special thanks to El Dopa.

Table of Contents:

GROWN ASS MEN

THE BIG CROSS

Carl was talking to his twin sister, Kate, who had dreamed of a glowing cross lighting up the desert.

"It's real," Kate said. "I Googled it. It's in Texas."

"It sounds like a coincidence," Carl said. It was 8:22 and time to make announcements at Irondale High, where he was the new vice principal and had once been known as Little Carl. He'd given up a job in administration at St. Louis Community College and moved back to the country to be with his sister. A year later she'd been diagnosed with ALS.

"It's huge," Kate said. "Skyscraper huge."

"Send me a link. I'll take a look."

"Just come over after work. I'll show you."

Kate and her husband Terry owned a small bar and grill. They'd done well enough, but Kate still liked to wait tables. Broke up the boredom, she said. Then her back started hurting, and she felt tired all the time. She told herself she was just getting old. Then she started dropping things, plates and trays, and her arms shook sometimes. She knew then what it was. It had killed Lou Gehrig and it had killed her mother and now, she figured, it was going to kill her.

Dr. Bremer said she could die within the year. "It's progressing quickly," he said. "But some people live a very long time. Stephen Hawking, for example."

"Who else?" Kate asked. "Name one other person." Dr. Bremer couldn't.

There had only been a ten percent chance Kate would inherit her mother's disease Dr. Bremer had said, and her bad luck filled her with, if not exactly pride, then a sense of destiny.

Carl arrived at his sister's house a little after four. His head hurt. He had suspended a kid, normally a quiet kid, a good student, for having half an ounce of marijuana in his locker. His girlfriend had ratted him out because he'd taken Amanda Green mudding in his pickup. The police had to be called and as the boy was being escorted away, his girlfriend came running out of Biology dragging her book bag behind her and screaming, I'm sorry, Tim. I'm so sorry. You can't be sorry enough, Tim said. But I forgive you anyway, baby. Sarah, Carl's secretary, thought it was sweet. For Carl it was just a big mess.

Kate was at the kitchen table with her poodle, Rocky, asleep at her feet and snoring—it had emphysema. Terry sat opposite Kate, his pie-face unreadable. His arms were thin and tattooed, and he was holding a cigarette that badly needed tipping. The table was covered in computer print outs of pictures and maps.

"Look," Kate said, pointing to a picture of the cross. It was white and an eighteen wheeler was parked at its base to give it scale. The picture had a smudged, surreal quality. "This is what I dreamt."

"You dreamed the picture or the cross?" Carl asked.

This stopped her for a moment. She tried to think of the right thing to say. She and Carl still looked a lot alike. Bright red hair, nearly six feet tall, broad faces and identical green eyes. Kate was still freckled, though not as heavily as when she was a kid.

Kate pointed at the picture of the cross again. "I know this is it. It's the second largest cross in the Western Hemisphere. It's 190 feet tall, can you believe that?"

Terry whistled, like you might if your dinner bill was fifty dollars higher than you thought it would be. Carl picked up Terry's pack of menthols even though he'd quit a few years earlier. He almost lit one, but thought better of it and slid them back toward Terry. He drummed his fingers against the coffee stained doily that covered the table. Kate hated that thing, but Terry's mother had made it for them as a wedding present. It had once been beautiful.

"We have to go," Kate said. "Right away." Her hands were shaky as she pushed the picture toward her brother. She assumed Carl would take her.

"I thought you were over all of this God stuff?" Carl said.

"I'm starting over," Kate said.

"It would be a nice trip for you and Terry. It will be good for the two of you to get away for a few days."

Kate snorted. "You don't believe me, do you?"

"I believe you had a dream, but it all seems odd."

"I can't go," Terry said, as if just realizing there was a conversation going on around him. "I need to watch the restaurant. Besides, I have no desire to go."

Carl looked back and forth between his sister and brother-in-law. They'd been married eleven years and never had children.

Kate took her brother's hand with both of hers. "We have to go," she said.

"What do you think, Terry?" Carl hoped for some measure of common sense.

"I think you're going to take her," Terry said. "So just agree to it and get it over with."

Carl took a personal day and arrived at his sister's house Friday morning. She was sitting on the couch in plaid pajamas. There was a brown suitcase beside her; they'd had it since they were kids. Although faded, the Transformers sticker Carl had put on it was still there. The trip would take close to eleven hours, and Carl planned to make it in one long stretch, get a hotel somewhere near

Groom, and be back home in plenty of time for Saturday Night Live.

"Are you going to get dressed?" Carl asked.

"It's a long drive," she said. "I may as well be comfortable, and it's not like I'm indecent."

Carl picked up the suitcase; it was heavy.

"What have you got in here?" Carl curled the suitcase like it was a barbell.

"Just stuff." She held the front door open for him. "You could use some exercise anyway. Do you think Sarah wants to go out with flab-o-arms?"

Kate's teasing had an edge. He'd had a crush on his secretary, Sarah, since his first week at work when she told Coach Brewer that if he called his new boss Little Carl one more time, she'd make sure his next check got lost. But despite his sister's prodding, Carl had never asked her out.

He stopped in the doorway, "Do you need to say goodbye to Terry or feed the dog or anything?"

"All taken care of."

They were backing down the driveway when the back tire raised slightly, and there was a brief, loud yelp. Carl put the car in park and it slid another foot, gravel crackling under the tires, before it stopped.

"I think I just backed over Rocky," he said. They got out to check. Kate was already tearing up and biting the collar of her pajamas. Fuck, Carl thought. Fuck. He pulled the dog out from underneath the car. Its midsection was flattened and the intestines had been pushed out, like corded ropes, from both the mouth and anus.

"Jesus," Carl said. "I'm so sorry, sis."

Kate bent over the corpse and stroked its head. Finally, she stood up, her eyes were red. "She was old and I think she had a good life, don't you?"

"Yes."

"There's a shovel in the shed. I can't leave her like this."

Carl folded his jacket neatly onto the back seat, rolled up his sleeves, and put Rocky in the Hefty brand garbage bag Kate brought him. It was a Cinch Sak, with a bright yellow draw string. As careful as he was, Carl ended up with blood on his shirt. It was late October and the ground was hard, but not yet frozen through. It took him forty-five minutes, and at one point he saw Terry's face, round and somber, staring out the kitchen window at him, smoking a cigarette.

"We'll have to stop by my place for another shirt," he said, handing the shovel to Kate when it was done.

"It'll dry," she said, and brushed at the blood stain as if she could wipe it away with her hand. "I'm begging you, Carl. I feel like I need to get there soon."

There was no place to stop on Highway 32, and by the time they reached I-44, it was eleven am. They stopped in Rolla for hamburgers. .

"What is that?" The blond girl asked, leaning out of the drive-thru window to point at Carl's shirt. Carl didn't know what to say. The long drive had lulled him into a fantasy world, and he'd forgotten about the stain.

"Ketchup," Kate said. "We tried McDonald's first. Awful stuff, messy."

"Oh," the girl said. "Actually, I prefer them. Here's

your food. You folks have a good day." As they pulled away, Kate patted her brother's thigh before leaning her head against the window and closing her eyes.

She didn't wake up until they were in Oklahoma. Carl stopped at a Wal-Mart in the very dry looking town of Glendale. Everything had a faint yellow tinge. It's just an illusion, Carl thought, dead and dried up grass, yellow and tan houses.

Carl shook his sister awake. "Can you get me a shirt?"

Kate stretched her arms, nearly poking her brother in the eye. "In my pajamas?"

"It's not like you're indecent," Carl said.

"Fine. What size and what kind?" Kate slipped on her shoes.

"Just get me a white one. They come in a plastic package and the brand name is George." Carl handed her some money.

Kate nodded and got out of the car. After about ten steps, she turned her head around, poked out her butt, and stuck her tongue out at Carl. Once she was out of sight, he took a book from his glove compartment— an old copy of Spider-man: Kraven's Last Hunt. He'd first read it in seventh grade, and had come back to it probably twenty times. He was lost in it when an old man knocked on his window.

"Hey," the man said. There was a black spot on his tongue.

Carl shook his head no. The man knocked again.

"I don't have any money," Carl said and waved the man away. He put his hand on the keys dangling from the ignition.

"I just need a dollar. I need to get to Texas. I have an aunt there. I need bus money."

"Go away," Carl said. "I don't have any money."

Carl saw his sister, a Wal-Mart bag dangling from one arm and her purse from the other. He started the car and rolled down the passenger's side window.

"Be careful, Kate," he said. She was approaching the man and digging through her purse for money. Carl opened his car door, pushing the man backwards with it.

"Hey," he said. "Be careful."

"I told you to go away," Carl said.

"I'm going to Texas," the man said.

"Me too," Kate said, as if that explained everything, and gave him ten dollars. He looked at it for a moment, stuffed it in his pocket and walked off.

Kate tossed her brother the Wal-Mart bag. He pulled a short sleeved, Hawaiian print shirt out of it.

"What this?" he asked.

"It was on clearance. Besides, I thought you'd look good in something with color."

"Damn it," Carl said. "Try to block me from people." He took off his blood-stained shirt. Kate stood facing him. The shirt was too small and stretched across his stomach. The gaps around the buttons hung open like mouths. Kate stuck her finger through one of them and poked Carl in the belly.

"You've put on a few. I can still fit in the same clothes I wore in high school, Little Carl."

Carl looked at his reflection in the car window. "I look like a tourist," he said. "A Glendale, Oklahoma, tourist. Well, screw it. Let's go."

In Tulsa, Kate decided she wanted a sit-down dinner. They stopped at Applebees and Carl ordered a steak and iced tea. Kate ordered a Miller Lite, no food.

"Is beer really healthy for you?"

"It relaxes my muscles." Kate fingered her hair, twisting it into red spirals. She was shaking.

"You're an adult. Do what you want."

Carl smiled at the waitress when she brought his food and ordered Kate another draft.

"She's pretty," Kate said. The girl looked to be in her early twenties, curly black hair, soft features. Carl nodded.

"You were looking at her," she said.

"I don't think so."

"How long's it been since you've been laid?"

"None of your business." Carl cut up his steak. He'd asked for it well done, but it was pink in the middle.

"Tell me it hasn't been since Belinda." When Carl didn't respond she said, "I bet it wasn't even good with Belinda. She was a cold fish. I could have told you it wouldn't work out."

"Then why didn't you?" Carl asked.

Kate shrugged. "You don't need someone as reserved as you are. You need someone like Sarah, don't you think?"

Carl didn't answer.

They turned west onto I-40, toward Amarillo. It was the last long stretch of highway before Groom. The sun had slipped into the horizon. Kate remarked on it. She thought the sun looked bigger in the west. Carl didn't notice a difference.

"Remember when we were kids and I was afraid to drive?"

"Sure," Carl said.

"Remember what you used to do?"

Carl gunned the engine and the car leaped forward.

"That's right," Kate said. "Used to scare me to death."

"Got you to take your driving exam at least."

"Not really. Sometimes I think part of the reason I put it off so long was because I loved the way it felt in your old truck on the back Irondale roads. I felt so out of control, so free. I loved it. I loved you and I knew you wouldn't let me get hurt."

"That was a long time ago," Carl said.

"Do it again. Please, Carl. There's not much traffic."

"It's too dangerous." Kate gripped Carl's knee. Please, she said again. One more time.

The '88 LaSabre didn't have the appetite for the road his old truck had, but Carl pushed down on the gas: 70mph, 80, 85. "Now," Kate said. Carl turned off the headlights. Kate squealed and buried her head in Carl's shoulder. Look, he said, look. Kate lifted her head and all she could see were the reflectors that divided the lanes. She felt like she was being shot through space.

The man Carl almost hit was pushing an empty wheelchair down the shoulder of the highway. Kate insisted they pull over. The man was in his mid-thirties, deeply tanned. He was short, wearing a tight white T-shirt and jeans; his muscles seemed to Carl like traps set on a spring.

"Careful there, fella," the man called out. "You could kill a guy driving like that."

"You were walking pretty close to the highway," Carl said.

"I guess I was. I've been walking a long way and you tend to lose track of things after a while. Then again you didn't have your lights on."

"Do you need a ride?" Kate asked.

"No way," Carl said.

"It's the least we can do," she said. "We almost killed him."

"I guess I could use a ride. I got business in Groom."

"So do we," Kate said. "That's where we're going."

"Look, I don't mean any offense," Carl said. "But we don't know you."

"You're good to be cautious," the man said. "These are troubling times. But I can assure you I'm on the Lord's work."

Kate put her hand on the back of her brother's neck, pulled him close to her and whispered, "It's a sign. Please."

Carl had never admitted it, but even more than sadness, which he did feel, he'd mostly been overcome by guilt since his sister had been diagnosed. It could have easily been him. It might still be him, although the odds were against it. He questioned himself every day since she'd gotten the news. He'd been at the doctor's office with her and comforted her when she turned to him instead of Terry. He had even gone so far as to write himself a message on a yellow Post it and stick it in his wallet: Am I wasting my life?

The man folded up the wheelchair, put it in the back of the car and slid in after it.

"Name's Bill Reilly," he said.

Carl waited with his blinker on at the shoulder of the road for a break in traffic. "Like the guy on Fox news," he said.

"That's O'Reilly." Bill leaned close to the back of Carl's seat. His cologne was strong and spicy. "O'Reilly's no Christian."

"You should put your seat belt on," Carl said.

"No need when you're riding with the Lord." Bill patted Carl's shoulder and then squeezed it.

"Just to be safe," Kate said, turning around to get a better look at Bill. "I'm Kate, and this is my twin brother, Carl."

Bill snapped his seat belt shut. "You don't look like twins," he said. "I figured you for a married couple."

"We used to look alike," Kate said. "Then he got fat. Believe it or not, they used to call him Little Carl."

"He looks like a little Carl," Bill said and removed a flask from the front pocket of his jeans. He took a drink. The smell of whiskey was strong.

"Hey now," Carl said. "You can't drink that in here. It's against the law."

"I follow God's law," he said. "Would you like a drink?"

"I'm driving," Carl said. His sister, however, politely accepted.

"That's good," she said, handing the bottle back to Bill.

"So," Carl said, "what exactly is this work you're on?"

"I'll tell you. I sell these wheelchairs. Been at it for about six months now. I do pretty good."

"Then where's your car?"

"Don't you worry about that, Carl." Bill said. "It's good fortune I was picked up by you folks, seeing as we're going to the same place. Yep, I knew Groom was the place for me as soon as I heard about that cross."

"That's where we're going," Kate said.

"That's a good sign. You're good people. I heard about the cross from a trucker. Sold him a wheelchair. His wife needed it."

"So what do you do when you sell one?" Carl asked. "How do you get another one?"

"Don't be foolish, Carl." Bill said. "This is just a model. When I sell one, I write the buyer's name and address down and have the company send it. It's an even split out of five-hundred. I guess I sell about ten a month. You could say I got the magic touch."

"You've got the magic touch," Kate said. Bill handed her the flask again, and she took a drink. "I had a dream about the cross. I saw it in a vision."

"I don't doubt it," Bill said. "I can sense these things. My mother called it the eye of God. Not psychic, mind you, that's Lucifer's work. I sensed something about you right away."

"I bet," Carl said.

"That's right, Carl. Anyway, that trucker told me there's God fearing folks in Groom, and I didn't take him for a liar. I do good business with Christians. They know they can trust me."

"I can see that about you," Kate said.

"Thank you," Bill said. "I get that a lot. Take two folks like you, a pretty lady and the meek type. You wouldn't just pick up anybody."

"I'm not meek," Carl said.

"Don't be ashamed," Bill said and patted Carl's shoulder again. "This is a sinful world and the meek will inherit it. I know you wouldn't just pick up anyone. They might be a killer or something worse. But you picked me up. It's a gift I have. It's the reason I got into sales."

"I almost hit you," Carl said.

"Have you always been a salesman?" Kate asked.

"I worked in a bank for a while, but it wasn't for me. I was called to the open road. I started out selling Jesus Mirrors. Those sold well, but I get more of a cut from the wheelchairs. I make a lot more money even though I don't sell as many of them. And there's no sin in it. A man has to eat. Ain't that right, Carl?"

"Jesus Mirrors?" Carl said.

"Yes, Jesus Mirrors, Carl. Mirrors with the face of Jesus painted on them. Some of them have a Bible verse. 'Yea though we walk through the valley of the shadow of death' was my big seller."

"Figures," Kate said. "It's just morbid enough."

"Not morbid," Bill said. "It gives hope. Sold good in Arkansas especially. They mostly hung them in the living room."

"Interesting," Kate said.

"Yes it is," Bill said. "Now, if you don't mind, I'm going to sleep for a bit. Don't you two worry. You're safe with me."

Kate slept as well. Eventually, Carl's eyes began to blur. He couldn't see the exit signs until he was right up on them, and the lights from the cars in the other lane blinded him. He was close to the Groom exit, probably seventy miles away, but he pulled into the next town anyway. He filled the car up with gas and then woke Kate and Bill.

"I can't drive anymore," Carl said.

"How close are we?" Kate asked.

"Close, but it's getting too dangerous. So unless one of you wants to drive we're going to have to find a place to stay."

"You know I can't drive," Kate said.

"I've been drinking," Bill said. "I don't have a license anyway."

Carl untucked his shirt and felt better. "We're going to have to get a hotel." Bill was already climbing out of the backseat, dragging his wheel chair with him.

"You good folks go on ahead," he said. "There might be some business here."

"What about the cross?" Kate asked. "Don't you want to see it?"

"I'll get there," Bill said. "I've troubled you all enough. You two be careful who you pick up. There are bad folks out there."

"We will," Kate said.

"There's a miracle waiting for you," Bill said. "Funny things happen when people get down this way."

"Thank you," Kate said.

"One more thing." Bill unfolded his wheelchair. "You all in the need of one of these?"

"No," Carl said.

They only rented one room because Kate didn't want to stay alone. Carl lay down immediately, taking off only his shoes. He told his sister it was fine if she relaxed with some television as long as she kept it low. He was tired, but when he closed his eyes he could still see the highway behind his eyelids. When sleep finally came, he kept moving down a dark, endless road.

He woke a few hours later feeling sick at his stomach. Motion sickness, he thought. The television was off, but the lamp beside his bed was on. Carl looked over to the next bed. Except for the suitcase, it was empty.

"Kate," he said. There was no answer. He stood up, fighting off a moment of disorientation, and checked the bathroom. She was gone. Taking his cell phone off the night stand, he dialed her number. A muted ring came from inside of the suitcase. Carl opened it.

Kate's undergarments lay on top, silky and frilly, the sort you would wear on a date. He picked them up, held them for a moment, and set them aside. He saw what made the suitcase so heavy. Crosses, a hundred or so of them—plastic, silver, ceramic. Some had the emaciated figure of Jesus on them, most were plain. What does she think is going to happen, Carl thought.

He found the phone; there was a new text message from Terry: I hope you and asshole are having a good time.

Carl put his shoes back on and went into the bathroom to splash water on his face. His eyes were red. He'd heard music when they were checking in and thought there must be a lounge. He found Kate there. She was sitting at the bar, wearing a red dress, cut low in the front, that brought out her hair and eyes. A drink sat in front of her, and she was talking to a young man. The lounge was crowded and the band had just started "Jessie's Girl" when Carl tapped her on the shoulder.

"Don't you think you're taking this drinking bit too far," he said.

"Carl," she said and wrapped her arms around his neck

.   "This is Jim. Right, Jim?"

"Jim," the young man said.

Carl nodded at him before turning his attention back to his sister. "Really, we should get back to our room."

"Just have one drink," Kate said.

"No, and you're not having any more either." He picked up Kate's glass. It looked like whiskey and coke. He handed it to the bartender.

"Hey now," Jim said. "The lady can have a drink if she wants one."

"This lady," Carl said, "is married. She's also dying."

Kate stood up and left without saying a word. Carl followed her to the room, but she wouldn't speak to him. She locked herself in the bathroom, and Carl could hear the muted sound of running water. He knocked on the door.

"I'm sorry," he said. "I didn't mean to say that."

"Fuck you," she said.

"Really. I didn't mean to. I'm sorry, okay?"

"And I said fuck you."

Carl took off his shoes again and set them beside the bed. It felt good to lie down. He was worried about Kate, he was sorry, but the sound of running water lulled him to sleep.

He could feel something stuck in his side. It tickled at first, but then it started to hurt. When he woke up, Kate was lying beside him and she had an inch of his fat between her fingers. She was squeezing so hard her face was red.

"I was drinking Diet Coke," she said. "And I was enjoying myself you self-centered cocksucker."

She sat up on the side of the bed and wobbled a bit before getting her balance. She was wearing a nightgown, white and sheer, with nothing underneath it.

"It's not like you haven't seen my tits before," she said. "Mother bathed us together until she died." Kate began to sob and her freckles blossomed into dark stars across her face. "I'm going to die too," she said.

Carl wanted to comfort her, but he didn't know what to do. He'd rehearsed this moment a thousand times in his head, and each time he'd said something profound. But now he found he could say nothing worthwhile.

"You're not going to die," she said. "Not you."

"I'm sorry."

"I believe you really are sorry, and I hate you for it." She lay down next to Carl, resting her head on his shoulder. They'd not slept like that since they were kids haunted by nightmares of their mother's death. Their father, Big Carl, had died a little bit with his wife and paid no attention to them. Carl had withdrawn from people, focusing on his schoolwork, while Kate, before her twelfth birthday, started doing meth. Carl found her using it half-naked with the old guy next door. He went back home, got his father's gun, and shot the man in the leg. The man couldn't report him, of course, and he moved shortly afterwards.

"And I'm going to be ugly, too," Kate said. "Twisted and ugly."

"No you're not," Carl said. "You'll always be beautiful. And there's still the cross."

Kate propped herself up on her elbow, leaned over Carl and kissed him. After a few moments, she stopped. "You kissed me back."

Carl didn't respond.

"I'm so sorry, Carl," she said. She stood up and went to her own bed. "You can't be in love with me. It's gross, and as you so elegantly put it, I'm dying anyway."

Kate was in a good mood the next morning. She hummed as she dressed. Carl was quiet and nervous. She finally sat down beside him, squeezed his hand and said, "Lighten up."

"You were drunk last night," Carl said.

"Seriously, lighten up. I worry about what's going to happen to you. I really do."

"Let's go to the cross. Let's just see what happens."

When they were 25 miles from Groom, they could already see the cross. It grew larger and larger until they found themselves in its shadow. The parking lot had a smattering of cars in it. The second largest cross in the Western Hemisphere did good business.

Carl parked the car. The cross loomed above them.

"It's now or never," he said.

"Wait," Kate said. "I have to say something."

"Go ahead."

"I slept with that guy last night. We did it in the back of the hotel, right in front of someone's door. We didn't even use protection."

"Oh."

"Do you think God will hold that against me?"

"I don't think so," Carl said. "Terry might." Kate dismissed it with a wave of her hand.

"Let's go," Carl said, pointing to the cross.

To Carl, once he was up close, the cross looked like a Titan from mythology—a giant with arms spread open. There was a plaque and a small statue of a baby at the bottom of it. Choose Life it read.

"It's a dilly."

"It's ugly," Kate said. "Just steel and white paint."

"I can't believe it. Look."

Bill was walking toward them, pushing his wheelchair and smiling. He waved.   Kate   reached out and touched the cross. She closed her eyes and after a moment withdrew her hand.

"Do you feel any different?" His voice was pleading.

"Today-day," she said, as if speaking into a great microphone, "I consider myself-self-self. The Luckiest . . ."

"Man man man," Carl said.

"Please Carl," his sister said. "Please."

He looked up. It was nothing but steel and white paint. Bill waved again. Carl waved back.

Mark called while I was looking through the junk drawer for something I could use to reattach the cover of my rotating fan. I was keeping my air conditioner off in an attempt to save money. My apartment was unbearable without at least circulating air, but I couldn't find the electrical tape.

"Jackson," Mark said. He sounded drunk. His New England accent heavier than usual.

"What's up?"

"She's going to leave me. Eli is going to leave me."

"What?" I tried to sound concerned, but the truth is I'd gotten this phone call before. Eli was going leave Mark for something or another about every six months or so.

"You know that girl I've been chatting with. The one who likes the band. Said she was going to interview me for a podcast."

I remembered. Her name was Gilda, or Glenda, something like that. She'd seen Mark's band, The Purples, playing around Manchester and later found them, then Mark in particular, on Facebook. They'd got to talking and the next thing you know she'd sent Mark a picture of herself in nothing but a corset and some frilly red and black underwear. He forwarded it to me. For him, she was an ego boost.

"What about her?"

"What's that noise?" Mark said.

I quit rustling through the drawer and closed it. I wasn't going to find anything for the fan anyway. I'd let it run without a cover until I could get to the Dollar Store for a new one.

"Nothing," I said. "Tell me what's going on. You didn't fuck her, did you?" The last update I'd gotten was that after the picture, Mark figured he'd crossed a line and he'd told Gilda or Glenda not to contact him anymore. She'd written back, asked him about the podcast, and they'd started back up again.

"God no. But Eli found everything. The emails, our Skype chats, everything."

"I don't even know how that is possible. You didn't delete stuff, clear browser history, anything?"

"I don't know, man."

"Did she say she wanted a divorce?" A horn squawked somewhere on Mark's side of the phone.

"You driving?"

"Crabby is."

"Good. You don't sound in the shape." I sat down in one of the two canvas camping chairs I'd set up in front of my TV and flipped on ESPN.

"What the hell is with the Pats?" I asked.

"Do you even care I'm getting a divorce?"

"You're not getting a divorce. If she's just thinking about it, it'll be fine. Right now she's at the height of her anger and she's just thinking. Just thinking, Mark."

"Yeah," he said. "She also called Doris." Doris is my ex-wife. "She told her everything." There was some rustling in the background on Mark's side. It sounded like a couple of chickens flapping around in a cardboard box.

"I gotta get off here," Mark said. "Crabby's lost and trying to read a map and drive at the same time."

"Use your fucking phone GPS?"

"Never!"

"Where are you guys?"

"Blytheville, Arkansas. We'll be there in about eight hours."

I tried to call Mark back several times, but he wouldn't answer the phone, probably because he knew I'd talk him out of coming. The apartment I'd moved into after I left Doris was one room, no curtains, and I was using a blow up mattress that I'd gotten at a yard sale for ten bucks as a bed. I'd rented my apartment because it was cheap and only a few miles away from Doris, but it wasn't the sort of place where one had company. There were a dozen or so empty Sprite cans on the counter next to the sink. For dishes, I just had one of everything—a plate, a bowl, a spoon, a plastic cup with one of those dudes from Twilight on it that had come free with a Big Gulp.

I hadn't seen Mark in a few years, Crabby in about six, and I wasn't sure I wanted to. I did, however, want to know what Eli had told Doris. I imagined she'd told her about every woman I'd slept with when we'd been married. There hadn't been a lot, but too many for a guy married just nine years. I'd only been divorced a month and I was worried. When Doris and I had split, I had the moral high ground, at least as far as she knew. I hadn't wanted the divorce even though I'd initiated it. I just wanted to make a point—stop sleeping with my cousin. Now, however, she would know better, and I couldn't imagine her letting it just roll off her back. Not after the guilt trips I'd laid on her. It's pretty easy to make a woman cry when she's in love with you and has fucked your cousin.

Sitting around and worrying about it wasn't going to help anything, so I decided, despite the Mississippi heat, I'd shoot a few hoops to pass the time. My basketball was in the closet, along with most of the other crap I never used anymore, stuff I had to step over when I was looking for a shirt. My apartment wasn't much, but the closet was a fairly big walk in—it also housed the water heater. I finally found the basketball under a pair of skis that I'd never used, but had refused to leave with Doris in case she decided to sell them, and it was surprisingly still holding air.

As I climbed out of the closet, my phone rang. It was Doris' ring tone—a snippet from Marvin Gaye's "Sexual Healing." I didn't answer. I wasn't ready for that yet. I wanted to talk to Mark first. I changed into a pair of basketball shorts. They were shiny and hung past my knees. At thirty-eight, I felt too old for them, but my other option was a stained pair of sweatpants that would be too hot to play in.

I hoped in my car, which I hadn't cleaned since the divorce. It had become infested with tiny, brown ants. I don't think they were fire ants because they never bit me. I didn't bother them either. It seemed like too much trouble and it would probably have been some kind of bad karma. They also kept me from having to drive what few friends I had in Mississippi around. No one wanted to ride in a car full of empty Sprite bottles and ants.

The basketball court was made of blacktop and I could see the heat coming off of it. After a few missed shots and long rebounds, chasing the ball off the court, I was out of breath and my knees were starting to hurt. I'd been a good athlete when Doris and I first got married, but I'd let myself go to hell. She tried to get me to exercise with her, and I always promised I would, but I didn't.

I'd met Mark and Crabby at the University of New Hampshire. I had wanted to get out of Mississippi so bad that I applied to the schools farthest away—Boston, NY, anywhere out east. Mark and I shared a dorm room, and we ended up forming a short-lived country band. We weren't bad. I had a hell of a voice, and Mark was a decent guitar player. There just wasn't much demand for country music around campus. We played a few small shows here and there, but we never got a crowd. Mark hated country music anyway. He was into hair metal, and I just couldn't get rid of my accent enough to make singing that sound anything other than sad.

Crabby had been friends with Mark since they were kids. They were both from Rhode Island. The three of us hit it off right away. We were all a little scared to be out on our own—like the freedom was too much for us, and at first it was. Too many nights drinking, smoking dope, looking for women (except in Crabby's case, but he'd still go along for the fun). I flunked out my third year, but Crabby and Mark made it. Mark, besides still playing in a cover band, teaches high school English. Crabby's parents left him a trust fund, and I cooked at an Applebees in Purvis, MS for four or five years, saved some money, married Doris, who'd also saved some money, and we opened a small bar and grill called The Pit. We made enough that we didn't have to worry about bills. We could even travel once or twice a year, and we were both happy with that.

I gave up on basketball after fifteen minutes. I was drenched in sweat and tired, so I decided to head back to my apartment to watch television. I hadn't been going into The Pit. Though we both still technically owned it, Doris had hired another cook and was doing most of the rest of the work herself. She sent me a little money every week. I grabbed my cellphone off of the front seat of my car, watched an ant crawl across my steering wheel, and saw that Doris had tried to call twice more while I was playing ball. I hit the call back button, let it ring once, and then turned my phone off. I'd have to face the music eventually, but not yet.

I still half-thought Mark and Crabby's trip was a joke. It's a hell of a drive and to not call me until they were in Blytheville was a sneaky move even for them. Then again, it was exactly the sort of thing we'd do when we were younger.

Mark called again just as the sun was going down, shining through my living room window in soft, purple strands. I threw my empty Sprite into the sink from where I sat. It was either a joke, or they were in town, and I didn't know which one I preferred.

"Hello," I said.

"We're in fuckin' Purvis," Mark said. "How do we get to your place?" I stood up, looked out my window. A group of kids were playing wiffle ball in the parking lot. Eventually someone, their mothers probably, would yell at them to watch out for cars or to come in because it was getting dark. The parking lot, the road beyond it, the strip mall beyond that. It all looked beautiful.

"It's easy," I said. "You're probably already on Main Street. Keep going until you see Fifth Street. Take a right. You'll see Pinewoods Apartments. I'm 12 B, second floor."

They arrived a few minutes later. I watched them pull into a non-visitor parking space, get out of Crabby's truck with a case of Miller Lite, and stumble up to my apartment. They knocked loudly, and I let them in. Crabby looked almost exactly the same. Handsome, sharp features. Red hair that was only now beginning to recede, a thick pair of curly chops I'd been trying to get him to shave since we were kids. He was a big guy that liked to dress like a lumberjack. Mark was thinner and now had streaks of gray in hair that fell past his shoulders. He was wearing a wrinkled White Snake T-shirt that looked to be a size too big. He had been doing yoga with Eli for the past six months and he looked fit. His jeans were faded with holes cut so perfectly in the knees you'd think he'd worn them out if you didn't know he bought them that way.

"This place is a hell hole," Mark said, looking around my apartment. "From the outside, it looks like a prison."

He had a point. The apartment complex was red brick, each room had only two windows, a big one in the living room, and one about the size of a sheet of paper in the bedroom. Both had dirty screens. The stairs, and the walkway on the second floor, were concrete in steel frames.

"I like to think of it as no frills," I said.

"That's about right," Crabby said and sat the beer down. "Want one?"

"No thanks," I said.

"Me either," Crabby said. "Give me one of those Sprites."

Then the awkwardness was over and we hugged. It really was good to see them. I told them to put their stuff wherever they wanted. They set it all down in the living room. I offered them the camping chairs, and I sat on a foldout stool I used when I was at my laptop.

"Got anything to eat?" Mark asked. "It's been a long ass drive. We never stopped except to piss and get gas. Just kept trading off back and forth."

"Not really," I said.

"Jackson's got nothing to eat?" Crabby rolled his eyes, and exaggerated gesture. "We've been talking about your cooking the whole trip."

"Eli's leaving Mark and you're all talking about my cooking. I'm flattered."

"I don't think she's going to leave," Mark said. "She thinks I'm an idiot, but she's forty years old with three kids from three different fathers. Who else would have her?"

"She's still pretty hot," Crabby said. "Somebody will fuck her."

"Fuck you." Mark sat his empty beer can down, and I picked it up and put it on the counter with my empty Sprites.

"So what we gonna do?" Crabby asked. This was a question I knew was coming, had prepared for even, but suddenly didn't have an answer for.

"I usually watch TV." It was on and tuned to ESPN. The only time it really left that channel were in the mornings when I watched the guy who used to be Regis and The View.

"Fuck television." Mark flipped his hair back in a practiced way.

"We could go grab something to eat, I guess. You need to tell me what all Eli told Doris anyway."

"In due time. Forget the food. What's that karaoke bar you're always talking about?"

"Yeah," Crabby said. "Haven't heard you sing in years, Jackson."

"Hey Jude's," I said.

"That's the one."

"The place where miracles happen," I said.

"What?" I was sure I'd told them this story before.

"It's just something the locals say. Anyway, sure. Why not?"

There was already a decent sized crowd at Jude's, there always was by the time karaoke started. What I liked most about the place is that there was no irony in it. It wasn't like some karaoke bars where everyone is trying to out do each other, or others where a bunch of hipsters get up and sing corny Conway Twitty songs badly just to make an angst ridden statement. Jude's brought in a crowd that actually liked to sing. Most of them weren't very good at it, but it didn't matter. They were appreciated anyway.

A short, potbellied man was standing at the front door of Jude's handing out tracts. He wore a St. Louis Cardinals hat and a trench coat that hung to the floor.

"Have you men accepted Jesus Christ as your personal savior?" he asked, before taking a sip of his drink.

"Of course we have," Crabby said, taking a tract with a badly drawn picture of the devil on it and pushing it down into his front pocket.

"Gabby's working," I said. Gabby had been mine and Doris' favorite bartender.

The three of us squeezed in between an elderly couple at the bar and ordered drinks. Mark got a beer, and Crabby ordered a rum and Coke.

"Hey, Gabby," I said. "I'll just take a Sprite."

"Do I know you?"

"I come in here, well I used to, come in here every Friday and Saturday night and sing with my wife."

She grunted, shrugged her shoulders, and handed me my drink.

Mark had already struck claim to a table and was halfway through his beer. Crabby and I joined him. The red vinyl cloth covering the table was sticky and every time we picked our drinks up, it would rise a few inches, clinging to the bottoms, before finally peeling off.

"This place smells like grease," Mark said.

"They cook appetizers and stuff in the back."

"I don't think I'd eat here. Maybe we can go to your place later."

"Probably not," I said.

I hadn't been to Hey Jude's since the divorce, but I saw familiar faces. I knew Bill, with the prosthetic leg, would sing "Copperhead Road." Claire would warble her way through "Walking After Midnight," perhaps twice if drunk enough. Mike would play pool all night, lose most of the games, and not clap for anyone.

"Well," I said. "What all did Eli tell Doris?"

"Everything," Mark said. "The nineteen year old, the waitress at your work, that other one."

"Damn it. Why can't you keep your mouth shut? I mean, why'd you have to tell her about all of that?"

"She's my wife."

"Maybe not for long," Crabby said. He picked up his drink, it came off the table cloth like a suction cup, thought better of it, and sat it back down. "I don't know why I ordered this. I'm just not feeling it tonight."

My phone beeped. It was a text from Doris. I opened it, no words, just a picture of a fat guy's bare ass, possibly mine. I got the point.

"What are you smiling about?" Crabby asked.

"Nothing," I said. "The singing will probably start soon." I nodded my head in the direction of the stage. It was small, and there was a black and orange Jagermeister poster, with a picture of a jack-o-lantern, covering most of the back wall. It had been there since Halloween.

"I'm not going to sing," I said. "Just so you know."

Mark sighed. "Jesus Christ, Jackson. You're a drag. We drive all the way here. No food. No singing. You're not even drinking, and this place you're always talk about is a dive. Even the bartender's fat."

Mark was just drunk, tired, and probably still worried about Eli, so I let his outburst slide and stepped up to the bar to buy him another beer.

"You sure you don't remember me, Gabby? I've only been gone about a month."

"Nope."

Mark apologized when I got back to the table. I'm a bit on edge, he said.

"What happened with you and Doris anyway?" Crabby asked. "You guys were perfect."

"She fucked my cousin," I said.

"That's it? Some cousin fucking. That can't be it."

"The cousin with the big schlong?" Mark asked.

My Sprite was empty and I didn't want to go back up to the bar, so I shook a piece of ice into my mouth and sucked on it.

"I guess it doesn't bother me much," I said.

"Bullshit," Mark said. "I'm worried shitless over Eli."

Crabby stroked his ridiculous sideburns. "What I'm saying is that these things are usually a two way street. People don't just cheat. There's usually something deeper."

"Now's not the time to go all gay on us," Mark said.

"I don't know," I said. "She just did it and then told me about it. I would have never known otherwise."

"How's your hog?"

"My what?"

"Your cock," Crabby said. "Maybe it's that." The stage lights went up, and Cat, the karaoke MC, welcomed us all to Hey Jude's and reminded us to tip our friendly bartender.

"We slept together our Freshman year," I said.

"We did?"

"Sort of." I couldn't tell if he was fucking with me or not.

"It must not have made much of an impression," he said. "That's probably it then. You just weren't doing it for her in the sack."

"Maybe."

"I just can't picture you two not together. I mean, I can't even imagine it." Mark said.

Cat welcomed Tim, Petey, and Corey, the guy who had been handing out tracts at the door, to the stage for an a capella performance of "Hush."

Mark wanted to know if they usually sang gospel at Jude's. Sometimes, I said, and sat back to listen. It was pretty good.

"This is just like that scene in Crossroads," Crabby said. "'Who's next? Who's gonna get their head cut?'" It had been one of our favorite movies in college, despite the constant smirk of Ralph Macchio.

"It's a bit creepy," I said.

Mark asked Crabby and I if we wanted anything from the bar, and when we both said no he made his way up there himself. I watched him. He looked like he'd been in a fight—shoulders slumped, walking like an old man.

"I guess this is pretty hard on him," I said.

"It happens all the time," Crabby said. "You know how those two are. Hell, they'll probably be together forever. Personally, I'm a bit sick of hearing him whine about it."

"Are you kidding me? When you and Jeff broke up we had to listen to you for months. Calling us in the middle of the night saying you couldn't sleep without him. Posting such gems on Facebook as, 'My rose is gone. My life is over.'"

Crabby laughed. "That was pretty fuckin' corny, but it was a long time ago."

"Last year," I said.

Corey and company were just finishing up when Mark got back with a beer and a shot. He offered me the shot, I refused, and he took it himself.

"I don't know what the fuck your problem is," Mark said. "You act like none of this shit with Doris bothers you."

"It doesn't," I said.

"The whore cheated on you."

Crabby shook his head no at Mark, but I told them both not to worry about it. Mark was never much of a drinker, but when he did he was always on the edge of belligerent.

"I cheated on her all the time."

"But she didn't know that." Mark said, throwing his hands up in the air.

"Maybe she did," Crabby said.

I'd never thought of it before, but he could have been right. Doris was sharp, always in tune with my moods. It was possible. Jude's was starting to get crowded, more crowded than I'd ever seen it, and the karaoke had gone back to tear in your beer songs and classic rock standards. A big guy, bigger even than Crabby, brushed passed me on his way to the stage. He wore a plain white T-shirt with a jean vest over it that someone had Bedazzled "Blackbeard" on the back, and he did have the blackest beard I'd ever seen.

"I think a raven died on that guy's face," Crabby said. "I wonder what he'll sing."

"It's raining men," I said. Crabby punched me in the arm—he was just joking around, but it hurt. It would leave a bruise.

"Gay jokes are so '90s," he said. Mark looked like he could barely keep his eyes open.

"Start the countdown," I said.

"Fuck you," Mark said.

"I give it two minutes." Crabby feigned setting his watch.

"I'll be fine. Even if Eli leaves me, I'll be fine."

It really was starting to get annoying. I excused myself to go the bathroom just as Blackbeard began his undeniably flat version of "Jesus is Just All Right With Me." The bar seemed hot as hell all of a sudden, probably the crowd. They had to be over the Fire Marshal's limit, but no one seemed to give a damn. I forced my way through them and toward the only bathroom. There was a short line of men, all older than me. I recognized one of them as Jim Brewer, a foreman at the Pepsi plant who sang nothing but Neil Diamond.

"Hey, Jim. Nice crowd tonight." Jim looked at me like I was nuts, nodded, and turned away to talk to the guy in front of him. By the time I got into the bathroom, I was about to pop. I figured I was going to be in there awhile, and thought about counting it out. When we were in college, it was something Mark did all the time. I'd hear him in the bathroom, pissing and counting, One Mississippi, Two Mississippi. The highest I ever heard him get was 73.

I had one hand against the wall, propping myself up as I leaned into the urinal. It wasn't sanitary, but I'd been having problems getting started. Something I needed to go to the doctor for, but just hadn't. The restroom was small, one stool and one urinal. The walls were white and encouraged graffiti. As I tried to pee, I read two versions of the timeless classic: Here I sit all broken hearted/ tried to shit/ but only farted. But what caught my eye looked like it had been written recently. The purple marker that had been used was still bright, and the handwriting was frilly, a lot of long strokes and loops. If thy right eye offend thee, pluck it out. I started to sweat, and I was pissing in stops and starts. It was painful. Someone kept knocking on the door, which wasn't helping. "What the hell are you doing in there," he said.

I finally finished, zipped up, and stepped back into the bar. A kid who looked to be in his twenties stood there. "Jesus," he said. "About time."

"I have a hard time pissing," I said.

"Sucks to be you then."

I was about to agree with him, but there was a of ruckus over at my table. Mark, Crabby and Blackbeard were jawing at each other and it looked pretty heated. A crowd was forming around them. I started that way, and then the karaoke stopped dead. I could hear them yelling at each other.

"This guy," Blackbeard pointed at Mark, "said it looked like I'd gone a little overboard with the Just For Men. Like I don't know what that means. This one," he pointed at Crabby, "is a fag." Crabby stood up. The top of his head came to Blackbeard's chin.

"So?" Crabby asked.

"Normally I wouldn't care, but your Yankee buddy here had to go and make a comment about my beard in his snooty Boston accent."

"I'm from Rhode Island," Mark said. Then he repeated himself very slowly. "Rhode Island. People from Boston say 'Pahk the cah in the Hahvahd Yahd.' We say, 'Pahk the ca . . .'"

"I don't give a fuck," Blackbeard said. "There's got to be recompense. Corey, hand me my chucks."

Corey of the religious tracks reached into an inner pocket of his trench coat, pulled out a pair of nunchucks and tossed them to Blackbeard.

"Holy shit," Mark said.

"Holy shit is right," Blackbeard said, but before he could do anything, Crabby pushed him to the ground, pulled Mark up from his seat, and drug him toward the door. I followed them out. I could hear Blackbeard asking Corey to help him up, and I knew it wouldn't be long until they were behind us. Luckily, Crabby had parked close to the entrance. I opened the passenger side door, Mark climbed in, and I slid in beside him, but Crabby was reaching for something in the bed of his truck. Even though it was dark out, there was enough light in the parking lot from the red neon Hey Jude's sign, that I could see what he had in his hands. It was a chainsaw.

"Fuckin' Jesus, Crabby. Put that thing down and let's get the hell out of here." I practically tumbled out of truck's cab, hoping I could defuse the situation.

"Fuck that," Mark said. He crawled out, fell, and started laughing.

Blackbeard, Corey and the rest poured out of the door, pushing and shoving each other—even Gabby was in the parking lot, leaving no one to watch the bar. I was pretty much just muttering, Jesus, Jesus, Jesus, over and over to myself. Mark was still on the ground laughing, and

Crabby was walking toward Blackbeard with a chainsaw in his hands.

"It doesn't have a chain," Mark said. "I don't even think it works."

Blackbeard was fluidly working the nunchucks behind his neck, under his arms, between his legs. Crabby raised the chainsaw, pretended to pull the cord, and yelled as loudly as he could, "Nun nun nun nun." It sounded nothing like a chainsaw. If anything, it was more like a kid trying to sound like a motorcycle, but Blackbeard's eyes widened and he nearly dropped his nunchucks before Corey said, "it's not on."

Blackbeard took a swing at Crabby. Crabby blocked the nunchucks with the guide bar, and pulled the chainsaw back over his head, taking the nunchucks with it.

"That's impossible," Blackbeard said. "I'm master of the Nunchaku." Crabby dropped him in three hits and looked at Corey, who raised his hands and shook his head.

"Good," Crabby said. "Everyone go back to their shitty singing." It took a few minutes, but they all did. Fights weren't that uncommon at Jude's. Crabby even helped Blackbeard up, patted him on the ass, and sent him back into the bar with a smile.

"Let's go," Crabby said.

"Back to Jackson's? I'm just getting started."

"Back to New England," he said.

"But what about Eli?" Mark bent over, putting his hands on his knees to hold his weight. Eventually, he was going to puke.

"That's the point," Crabby said. "You didn't even tell her where you were going. I don't know what in the hell we were thinking. It's been two days."

Mark nodded. "I just want to go to sleep," he said. "Get back home, see my son." Crabby helped him off the ground and into the truck.

"You coming, Jackson?" he asked.

"I think I'll stick around here for a bit. You guys going to be okay?"

"Yeah, but do you mind if we sleep at your place for a few hours before we take back off?"

"Not at all." I handed him my key. "Stay all night. We'll go to the Waffle House in the morning before you take off."

"Sounds good," Crabby said.

I sat at the bar for a while and drank Sprites. When Doris called again, I answered.

"Well," I said. "I guess you know everything now."

"I guess I do," she said.

"Are you mad?"

"Yeah."

I missed her voice. I didn't even realize it until I'd heard it again. "You want to meet me at Jude's?"

"No," she said. I motioned for Gabby to bring me another Sprite. Corey sat down beside me, looked like he was about to say something, and closed his mouth when he saw I was on the phone.

"I'll wait here for a bit just in case," I said.

"Don't hold your breath, darlin.'" Corey slid a tract across the bar to Gabby. She waded it up and threw it in the trash.

"Mark and Eli are getting a divorce," Doris said.

"For real?"

"For real."

"Damn," I said. We stayed on the phone for a bit, neither of us saying anything, before I hung mine up without even saying goodbye. When Doris walked through the door, a cool breeze came with her. It was raining outside. I was in a heated debate with Corey over existentialism that Doris put a quick end to by asking him to move. She sat down beside me. She was wearing my favorite dress.

"What do you want to sing?" she asked.

"It's up to you."

Gabby, without asking Doris what she wanted, fixed her a slow gin fizz. Then she looked at me. "I remember you now," she said. "You cook over at The Pit."

TWO MONTHS BEFORE, TWO MONTHS AFTER

Chip sat at the far end of the bed, away from Lynn, rubbed his eyes, and listened to her snore. Willy, his dead father's dog, trotted over and looked up expectantly. Chip patted him on the head and pushed him away. The dog was big, 68 lbs, sandy, and a long tongue covered in purple spots. He had a long snout Chip sometimes grabbed if the dog was humping company or chewing up furniture. Leonard, Chip's father, had refused to have the dog fixed. He'd say, "You don't cut off balls like that." It had driven Chip's mother crazy.

It was late. Chip yawned. Pushing the dog away again, he stood up and looked for the underwear he'd kicked off the night before. They were tangled under Lynn's feet; Green things with gray stripes that she'd picked up because she thought they were fancy. If he didn't wake his wife, and if he hurried, he'd have about fifteen minutes to drink coffee and play his game.

As Chip reached for the underwear, the dog clamped his teeth onto them. Chip pulled, Willy shook his head and growled. Chip pulled harder. The dog lowered his head, ass in the air, and set his feet. Trying to wrench them free, Chip dragged Willy across the floor. The dog's long claws left trails in the varnish. The snoring continued.

It was January, northern Michigan, and their house was old. Chip grabbed the dog's snout and squeezed until it unclenched its jaws. Chip had one leg in when Willy gave it one last relentless attempt. The dog bit down, bit again, and pulled his head away with a snap. Where Chip's penis had been, flaccid and splotchy, there was only blood. It splashed upon the olive curtains and pooled sloppily upon the painted windowsill. The dog swallowed, without even bothering to chew. Chip fell to the floor. It was the reddest blood he'd ever seen; his brother had owned a Camaro that exact shade when they were kids.

Two months before.

1. Lynn.

Chip and Lynn were making love. It was hard work. They'd been going at it for half an hour, first with Lynn on top, then Chip. It was cold; snow fell outside the bedroom window, a television tuned to fog. Both were sweating, and she kept pushing and slapping at his hips, trying to get him to adjust to her speed. He'd had four glasses of wine at dinner, two past his usual limit, and could barely stay hard, much less come. He tried thinking about other women, but it didn't work. He pictured his wife with another man, a younger, smooth bodied man, with a monster prick. The image was vivid and helped. Lynn started breathing heavily. Her hands clenched at the sheets. And then it was done.

After Chip came, he rolled over, breathing heavily. The guilt was palpable and it lay between him and his wife like a sleeping animal.

"Did you come?" Chip asked. He knew she hadn't.

"No, honey." Lynn rolled over on her side, wiped a strand of limp white hair from her round face and kissed her husband's shoulder. Her breath was hot and smelled of fruity wine.

"Do you want me to do anything for you?" Chip asked. It was after ten and he'd have to be up for work by 5:30.

"It's ok. I'm pretty tired." She smiled and nestled her head into the crook of his elbow. It was their 19th anniversary. They'd had a nice dinner at Red Lobster, Lynn's favorite. She had worn a short red dress and Chip had commented on her eyes. She had smiled when he'd given her a gold bracelet. Her toenails were painted, and she wore open toed shoes, despite the weather. The snow had started to fall on the way home. The road quickly turned white, and it took them forty five minutes longer than usual. It was the thing she most hated about Michigan.

"I wish you'd let me." Chip said. He knew he'd not be able to get it up again, but he could do something. Wanted to do something.

Barely shaking her head, Lynn mouthed "no." The type of exaggerated no that could mean anything.

"I don't mind." Chip said. "I really don't."

"I want to just lay here for a bit."

Chip reached over and clicked on the nightstand lamp. It cast a soft glow over the bed, and Lynn pulled an olive green cover up to her chin. Chip asked her to give him a look, and tried to pull the cover back off of her. They'd wrestled over that for a bit, laughed for the first time that night, but eventually Lynn won out. Propping himself up on his elbow, Chip leaned over to kiss her.

"Really, let's just lay here," she said. "It's nice."

They lay in silence for a bit and he watched the snow fall until it made him dizzy. Lynn sighed almost inaudibly.

Chip rolled out of bed and found his boxers.

"You're not coming to bed?" Lynn pressed her lips tightly together and a web of wrinkles spread across her face. It was, for Chip, a condemnation. He could taste her disappointment.

"I'm going to take the dog out."

Lynn lay in bed, tightly wrapped in her blanket. Chip stood over her, naked except for his black boxers. They both expected the other to speak first.

"You're going to play that game again," Lynn said. "And you have to work in the morning."

2. Penny

Penny's head rested on Chip's chest and her hand stroked his hairy stomach. She'd come hard, twice. It had always been easy for her, even the first time in the back seat of Bill Sutton's Cutlass. She'd thought that rusty thing would fall right off the axles.

They were, as always, in her apartment. A one bedroom in Saginaw—the walls were white and the landlord wouldn't let her paint them. It didn't bother her. Chip had offered to take her shopping for plants, knickknacks, something, as long as they didn't spend too much money. But she'd told him not to waste his time. She was happy with a few ferns, a fish bowl, her laptop.

"Do you love me?" She asked.

"Oh Jesus," Chip said. "Here it comes."

"What?" Penny reached down and squeezed his limp penis. "Tell me or I'll rip it off."

"Come on, Penny. Really." Chip shifted his weight to his left side; he'd gotten his legs tangled up in the flower print bedspread. He was almost positive it was the same bedspread his grandmother had once owned.

"I love you," she said. And she did, although she hated him sometimes, too, which seemed natural enough to her. But she figured, rightly, that Chip wouldn't understand her on that level. The first time they'd met, she'd felt an overwhelming desire to take care of him. She had expected that to pass, but it hadn't. It had just grown into an uncomfortable beast.

"I know you do. But I'm not leaving my wife."

Penny sat up, pulled on Chip's AC/DC T-shirt and lit one of his Pall Malls. She inhaled sharply.

"Goddamn it, give me that." Chip snatched the cigarette from Penny's mouth and stuck it in his own.

"You can't smoke."

"I know that. But you piss me off." She reached again for the pack, but was too slow.

"I piss you off?"

"I didn't ask you to leave your wife. I've never asked you to leave your wife. Stop making me feel like a whore."

Chip sighed; he'd not meant to make her feel that way. He looked around the room; it was so bare it made him feel claustrophobic. Everything was white—the walls, the carpet, sterile as a hospital. "Why don't you get a goddamned clock?"

Penny rolled her eyes. "Look," Chip said, "I didn't mean it like that, ok?"

He tugged at the faded T-shirt until Penny relented and lay beside him again. He put the cigarette out in an empty Budweiser bottle sitting on a plastic white, pop up table near the bed.

"I just want an answer," she said. "It's not going to make a difference either way. Do you love me or not? It's a fair question."

Eventually he'd have to say it whether he meant it or not. It doesn't even matter if you mean it, he thought. Saying it is close enough.

"Yeah," he said. "I guess I do." If he wasn't careful, he thought, he might start to believe it.

Chip felt Penny relax and she snuggled in close to him. "What do you love about me?"

Chip shrugged. He didn't even know where to begin answering a question like that.

"I'm serious. Just tell me. Make it up if you have

to. I don't care. Just say something."

"I love your boobs."

"That's a given" Penny said. "What else?"

"I like your big ass."

"Oh, fuck you, buddy."

"I'm serious. I've sworn off little asses."

Penny rolled over on her back, using Chip's fleshy arm as a pillow and glared at the white ceiling. Chip felt the need to do something.

"I love this," Chip said, and traced the cesarean scar at the base of her stomach with his finger. He felt clumsy.

He wasn't the greatest looking man, Penny thought, although he'd probably once been handsome. You couldn't call his stomach a beer belly, but it sagged. His hair had started to thin and go gray. He never cut his toenails and she could barely bring herself to look at them. But the sex was good, he appreciated her, his pure thankfulness was overwhelming, and there was always the game.

"Did you level last night?"

"Yep," Chip said, glancing toward the door. It was made of cheap wood, painted white, and there was an indention in the center of it the size of a fist. He had never asked her anymore about that than he had her scar.

"You going to be online later?" Chip asked.

"You know it." Penny reached across him for her glasses.

He heard: A wailing siren. A screaming wife. Something about ice. A deep male voice. Lynn: I didn't do it. It was his dad's dog. He inherited it. He smokes, but only after. After.

One month before.

1. Lynn, Troy and the Game.

The game wasn't even trendy and there were no graphics. It was just an old fashioned text MUD. At most there were 600 players. Some kid at the factory had talked about it nonstop. It got on everyone's nerves. But, bored one night, after fighting with Lynn, Chip decided to check it out. They'd recently bought their first computer and he'd been chided for not showing much interest in it. You need a hobby Lynn told him.

It took him a bit to get used to the scrolling text; it was hard to keep up. But he liked figuring things out, and soon the world opened up, as if someone had removed a blindfold from him, and when he looked at clock in the corner of the screen again it was 3am.

When he first started playing, Lynn thought it was cute. At 42, he was boyish, eager when he played. He'd talk to her about the levels he had gained, what mob he'd killed, how far he had advanced. When she'd told him about Troy she thought that part of him had been lost. Troy from work, he'd said, that kid. She nodded and waited for the explosion, but it never came. He sat on the couch and asked her to tell him what happened. His desire, she thought, no his craving for every last detail unsettled her. You didn't sleep with him, he asked. She hadn't. So you kissed him, he said, and he felt you up. She nodded, again. And you grabbed his cock? She was crying, but his voice was emotionless. They had been going over it for two hours. Well, how was it, he said. Big? Average? She had screamed at that point and he stopped. He put his arm around her and told her that he was sorry, and that had made her scream again because she knew that he was and that her sorry had been swallowed by his.

It may have all ended up good even then, she thought, it would be a scar but it would heal. And then that bastard father of his died and then he started playing that game non-stop. It was the first thing he did in the morning. It was the last thing he did at night. Half of the time he played through dinner, his plate in front of him next to the computer. If she didn't know any better, she could have sworn he was addicted. But that was ridiculous. People don't get addicted to games, least of her husband.

But it seemed to make him happy. So when he talked about it, she smiled and nodded and joked about having married a geek. Sometimes she'd open a bottle of wine and ask him to play his guitar and he'd fumble through something by Springsteen or Neil Young. He'd rush through the songs thinking only of dragons, sirens and magic. Later, when she was watching Letterman, he'd pour himself a glass of tea and play. She would sleep, and he'd wake up for work late and tired.

2. Penny and Jewel.

He had met Penny in a dungeon. Her in game name was Jewel. She was in his guild, a warlock. They'd been surprised to discover they lived only two hours apart. It's a small world, she said, but then again, what else you going to do with winters like these? That had intrigued Chip and soon they married in the game. Role playing— the gamers called it RP.

Half a year later, they met in real life at the Renaissance fair in Holly. It was May, but still cool enough for a jacket. He had not dressed up as many of them had like bards or priests or knights, but in faded jeans, flannel and tan boots. He told Lynn he was just going to check it out. She didn't understand, but she didn't stop him either. At the last minute he'd felt a tinge of guilt and had asked her to come with him. She refused even after he asked her to look at is as a second honeymoon. I get enough of that game, she said.

Penny wore tight Wranglers. Her black hair was braided and her glasses kept slipping off of her nose. There was a mole on the back of her neck that she'd need to get looked at someday. Even in that baggy sweater she looked pretty stacked, Chip thought, and choked back a pang of guilt. He felt awkward, like he was being watched, and was thankful when Penny took control of the conversation. They drank in the beer garden and when talk lulled, Penny brought it back to the game and smiled at the way she could physically see him relax.

Chip invited Penny back to his hotel. She kept her shirt on as they made love; when she came the first time she collapsed beside him and all he could do was stare at the swirling white patterns painted on the ceiling and wonder why he didn't feel nearly as guilty as he would like to. After Penny was asleep, he called his wife and told her that he'd be home early. The next night, while Lynn slept, he slew his first dragon.

It was gone. Lynn had waited, near panic, as the EMTs gave the dog a dose of peroxide. It began to vomit almost immediately. But it had been too long. It was too mangled.. When Chip, high on pain killers, asked, she said, "It's not a diamond ring dear. It's gone." She held his hand and cried for him. Their only daughter, Sally, had moved in with her boyfriend six months earlier. She refused to visit. "Imagine how weird it must be for her," Lynn said.

One month after.

1. Bruce, Lynn and the fish.

Chip wouldn't answer the phone when his brother's name, Bruce, showed up on caller ID. He had been calling for days, and Chip knew that Lynn had been talking to him behind his back, but he wasn't ready. It might be good for you to talk to him, Lynn said. But all Chip could think about was that his little brother still had a penis and he did not.

Lynn worried. Now that he wasn't working, Chip played his game more than ever. She could no longer bring herself to complain about it. She tried getting interested in it. She would peek over his shoulder as he typed and he would close the screen and pretend to look at porn. She had asked him if she could watch and he had said, no, it's embarrassing and she didn't push it any farther.

He wouldn't see a psychiatrist, but she had started seeing Dr. Kennedy. She had told Lynn that Chip was bound to be depressed, and that unless he started to have thoughts about hurting himself that he would eventually work it out on his own. If the game helped then let it help, she'd said. Lynn tried to explain that he'd been playing it before, but Dr. Kennedy was more interested in talking about Lynn's feelings. On the lost penis she could only say, he'll deal with it in his own way.

Lynn wasn't satisfied with that. So she had started talking to Bruce. He and Chip had always been close. If she could just get Chip to talk to him, another male, maybe it would help. She had only let Chip refuse for so long. On the morning Bruce arrived, there had been a quite a scene. The brothers nearly came to blows. Their faces were red from screaming, but Chip finally backed down and agreed go ice fishing with his brother. Bruce had already packed the gear in the bed of his truck.

They went to Higgins Lake. Bruce had set the shack up earlier in the winter. Their father had built it, and they'd been using it since they were boys. Bruce drilled a hole through the ice with the hand augur they had always used. It was part of the tradition. Chip didn't help, nor did Bruce ask him to. He drilled in silence. When he was done, he sat down beside Chip, wiped the sweat off of his face with an old rag, and pulled a pint of Jim Beam from his backpack. It went down smooth and he handed the bottle to his brother.

"So, what did you drag me all the way out here for again?" Chip asked and took a small drink straight from the bottle.

"We haven't been fishing all winter," Bruce said. "Hell, I've only seen you in the hospital and you wouldn't talk to me then."

"Bullshit. You and Lynn conspired to get me out here, so just cut to the chase, ok?"

Bruce dropped his line. He might hook a Walleye or a Pike, but he wasn't concerned either way. "I'm just worried about you, that's all."

"I'm fine," Chip said and took another sip of whisky. He'd have to make sure to be careful. Bruce, if tradition held, would end up too drunk to drive.

"Lynn doesn't seem to think so. She thinks you're far from fine."

"I wish you'd quit calling her."

"She calls me. She needs someone to talk to."

"She can talk to me." Chip wanted to smash his brother's face, but he was sure he wouldn't be able to take him anymore. Bruce was only a year and a half younger, but he'd aged better. His shoulders were still broad and his stomach tight.

"Right," Bruce said. "Right."

"Is this about that stupid game? Fine. I'll quit playing. It's not that much fun anymore anyway. It's just something to do." Chip reached across Bruce's line for the bottle of Beam.

"It's a sight more than that," Bruce said.

"I lost my dick, Bruce. Give me a break. Both of you. Give me a goddamned break."

"I know, bro. And I'm sorry. I can't even imagine. But if you don't get a hold on yourself you're going to lose a lot more than that."

Chip sat his pole beside his feet. He didn't feel like fishing. He didn't feel like talking either, but it didn't look like he was going to get much of a choice. He took another drink. It would be his last one; it had already gone to his head. They sat in silence for a while.

"I know about that girl you have," Bruce said. His pole had bent once and he'd cut the line and sat it next to him. He was not there to fish.

"What?" Chip felt a rush of adrenaline, the first since the accident, it filled him with pleasure.

"Fuck," Bruce said. "Don't play this game with me."

"Well then, what about it?" Chip turned the battery operated space heater up to eight.

"Lynn knows too. She's known since before the accident."

Chip sat with his elbows on his knees, staring at the ice.

"She's not stupid," Bruce said. "For as much time as you spend on it, you don't know jack shit about computers. You leave AIM up, you don't log out of your email. It's like you wanted to get caught."

"Why hasn't she said anything?" That angered Chip the most. Lynn would tell his brother, but not him. He knew that later it would be guilt, but for now, it was just anger.

"Why hasn't she said anything? Hell if I know. Probably because she loves you. Because you're forty-two years old and never been with another woman. Because you've always been the perfect husband. Jesus, half the time I get the feeling you shit rose petals."

"I'm ready to go home," Chip said.

"We're not going anywhere until I've had my say."

Bruce offered the bottle to Chip, but Chip refused it.

"Then have at it," Chip said.

"Ok. Look, I don't know if you're going through some mid-life fucking crisis or if you're just as depressed as everyone keeps saying you are, but it's time to buck up."

"And I should be taking advice from you?" Chip couldn't bring himself to raise his voice. There was no denying it. He was afraid of his brother.

"Same old shit, huh?" Bruce took another drink. "I can't hold a job. I can't keep a woman. That's fine, bro. That's the way I'm built. Like dad without the sense of responsibility. But I'm happy. I don't make a pretense and I don't hurt anyone. You're killing everyone around you. Sally won't even come to visit."

"It must be hard on her," Chip said.

"You're making it hard on her. Get your head out of your ass. Break it off with that bimbo and get your life back together."

Chip swung at his brother and caught his left cheek with a glancing blow. Bruce wobbled, nearly fell off of his chair, but regained his balance. He was on Chip like an animal and had him pinned to the ice before Chip could make another move.

"Fuck you," Bruce said.

2. What happens at Higgins Lake stays at Higgins Lake.

Chip returned home with a black eye and a busted lip. Lynn fretted, ran a wash cloth under hot water and tried to wipe the blood off of her husband's face. Chip pushed her away. The attention she paid to him just made it worse, like she was his mother. He had just had his ass whipped and wanted nothing more than to go to sleep.

Things had changed in a way that he could feel at the core of his soul. Lynn loved him and he loved her. But it had all gone to hell. He couldn't let her love him anymore. Not unless something changed.

Two months after.

1. How to almost save a marriage.

There was just nothing there. A scab like a severed umbilical chord, a hefty nut sack, and an empty space that just didn't seem empty at all. Chip still wanted sex. He still dreamed of it. His balls hurt with it. They were heavy with semen. At the Lion's Den, he fumbled with various lubes, calendars, decks of dirty playing cards, until a pretty pink haired girl behind the counter asked him if he needed help. Hell yes he needed help. He came home with sixty bucks worth of top of the line strap on.

That night he fucked Lynn violently, pinning her to the bed, biting her shoulder, gripping her wrists until her hands turned purple. By then, he'd already shot the dog and buried it in the back yard underneath a willow tree. When Lynn tensed he asked her if she was coming.

"Yes," she whispered.

"Are you fucking coming," he asked.

"Yes," she said.

2. Any port in a storm.

Chip sat at Penny's desk in front her computer. Since the accident he'd spent nearly two hundred hours of in game time. There's just nothing there, his wife had said. And when he dreamed, he dreamed of sex. He dreamed of fucking his niece, his mother, his seventh grade art teacher, Ms. Henderson, whose breasts sagged to her navel when she sat.

Lynn had started to dote on him. He'd went to shovel the snow, and found the boy up the street had already been hired to do it. He wanted to put in a new sink, but she insisted he let her call a plumber. She fixed dinner everyday, and sometimes wiped his mouth with the corner of her napkin.

Lynn hadn't packed up and left on her own, but he'd asked her to go when she stopped letting him use the strap on. By that time, he had taken to wearing it around the house. Holding up her arms Lynn had said, "Look at this. And this. And this." Purple and yellow splotches. Fireworks. The phone rang, work, but he wasn't going back.

Penny, fresh out of the shower, coughed. Chip looked up expectantly. Her bush was wild; her tits covered in droplets of water. She wore nothing but a latex glove, and she held a bottle of baby lotion.

She was pregnant. The scar on her stomach was puffy and red from the heat of the shower, but she wasn't yet showing.

"What are doing?" Chip asked.

"C'mere, old man. I'll show you." She arched a sharp eyebrow. Afterwards, maybe they'd go shopping and have a nice dinner.

INNER CHARLIE

When Charlie woke up he couldn't find his inner Charlie. It was the damn alarm clock again. Every morning it woke up Charlie. Every morning he couldn't find his inner Charlie. Maybe he would go to the bar. Sometimes it helped and sometimes it didn't. "Charlieeeeee," he yelled sounding just like the old Warner Brother's cartoon women who screamed for their children. Nothing happened.

Charlie took a shower. The water rolled off his Charlie in tiny beads. He dried. Then he brushed his Charlies. The bar, yes, the bar would help this morning.

He thought he'd put on some nice disco clothes. Then he put on some nice disco clothes. Yeah, lookin' very Charlie today. But, as any Charlie will tell you, lookin' Charlie and bein' Charlie are two different things. Charlie jumped into his 2013 Charlie convertible and rolled down the street. Funky, Charlie, Funky!

The bar had a nice scene goin' on for a Charlie morning. The beatniks and artist would be there. Charlie ordered a Charlie on the rocks. He noticed some Charlies he knew sittin' in the corner, drinkin' Charlies and wearin' their disco clothes. Funky, Charlies, Funky!

He joined the Charlies. "Hey, Charlie, how you doin'? How 'bout you Charlie?" "Fine," said the Charlies, "how are you Charlie?" All right I guess, but I'm havin' a hard time findin' my inner Charlie this morning." The Charlies nodded in grave understanding. "Have another Charlie maybe that will help." Charlie ordered another Charlie and knocked it back.

"I'm working on an interesting poem. It's called "Charlie," said Charlie.

"Yes, my novel, Charlie, is coming along well, Charlie."

"I was working on a play until my Charlies kicked me out of the house."

"That is so un-funky, Charlie."

"I know, Charlie."

"My painting of the Charlies is complete. I hope to sell it to a rich Charlie soon."

"Charlies, my inner Charlie just isn't comin' today. I think I'll go home and sleep."

"Un-funky, Charlie, un-funky."

"You know what it's like when you can't find your inner Charlie, Charlie, you get all Charlied out in no time."

"I've never understood gettin' Charlied out, Charlie, I'm all funked up with Charlie. It is the basis of my poetic philosophy. I live to Charlie. I am a Charlie. It eats at my very Charlie soul in a way the non-Charlies will never understand."

The Charlies all nodded solemnly in agreement.

"You guys are all so Charlie. I don't know how you do it."

"Are you sayin' that you ain't Charlie?"

"No, Charlie, I'm Charlie all the way but sometimes I just wonder if there is more to life than Charlie."

The Charlies gasped in disbelief.

"Charlie, you've gone un-funky. You need to quit talkin' like that or go. We can't have the Charlies on our backs for bein' unfunky and hangin' with a non-Charlie."

"NO, Charlie," Charlie said suddenly afraid of the respect he could lose, "I'm Charlie, Charlie. I ain't gonna wander from my Charlieness. Charlies everywhere will envy my Charlieness. I'll be back on top I just need to find my inner Charlie and I'll be the Charliest again."

"Well, until then amscray arlychay."

Charlie turned, head down.

"Wait, Charlie," The Charlies said, "We forgot somethin."

The Charlies took turns kicking Charlie in the Charlies until he cried. Then they threw him out back in a dirty alley, where no Charlie would ever be caught dead. Charlie brushed himself off, looked around at the bums, and ran.

Charlie left the scene. It was not funky to be so un-Charlie around the Charlies. He didn't know what had come over him. He was empty. He needed rest. He hadn't written a Charlie worth a damn in weeks. He had heard that sometimes medication was enough to bring back one's inner Charlie but he was still a little too Charlie to try it.

Charlie's dog, Charlie, was funked up when Charlie got home. He fed him some Charlie brand dog food then sat down.

"Charlie, it must be nice to be so blissfully Charlie," Charlie said before he Charlied his way back into his Charlie for a nice long Charlie.

Before Charlie feel asleep he found himself wondering what it would be like to be a Henry or a Mike. He wondered what they did when they hung out. Would it be at a farm? A discount store? Maybe at a bar, but certainly not at the bars the Charlies Charlied around in. It's crazy talk, Charlie. Henrys and Mikes are just too un-funky, too redneck. But, certainly there had to be some Mikes who wrote just as well as Charlies. No, if there were the Charlies would have told him about it in Charlie school. No, The Henrys, Mikes and Randolf's just weren't Charlie. They were toto un-funky.

When Charlie awoke he couldn't find his inner Charlie but he felt like he was coming closer to it. He Charlied out of his Charlie, grabbed himself a Charlie, and headed out the Charlie with a Charlie-eating-Charlie wide across his Charlie. Yes, he was a Charlie and he'd hang with the Charlies. It was his destiny to write the Charliest Charlies of them all and no Tom, Dick or Harry could stop him.

THIS LOVE STORY HAS A ZOMBIE IN IT

It's a little after nine at the Shamrock. It's just the workers—me, the bartender Trish, Linda, tonight's waitress, the cook, Charlie, and our boss, Hunky. I'm taking a break from the dishes, having a cigarette at the bar and talking to Trish when my brother's fiance walks in. My brother has been dead for almost twenty years so she has a man with her. I recognize Vicki right away. Her blond hair is still a wall of Aquanet. A scar like a starfish on the left of her chin, starting just under the lips and stretching to the middle of her neck. I put out my cigarette, get off of my bar stool and go back to the kitchen, looking for dishes to wash. We're slow and there aren't any. I take a wire scour and scrub the grime off of the dishwasher. It doesn't take long. I'm good at my job and I keep the place pretty clean.

I've already changed the grease in the fryers and stocked the walk in. Charlie is out back in his "office" getting high. It's June, a Friday night, the kitchen is hot and we're dead. Hunky will want me to clock out soon. I walk to the door separating the kitchen and the bar, the green paint is flaking off of it, and look out the small, greasy window we use to make sure we don't hit each other on the way in and out—it doesn't always work—I've been knocked in the head several times with it. Vicki is sitting at the bar, a Bud Light in front of her, smoking a menthol alone.

"Boo," Charlie says, squeezing my sides in his big hands.

I jump. "Holy fuck," I say. Charlie is burnt, marble eyed. He's wearing a sleeveless shirt and he has a fucked up American flag tattoo on his left arm. The lines aren't even straight and we counted the stars on it at 49 one night.

"Let's have a beer," he says. We always get a few free after work, more if Hunky is drunk, which he usually is.

I don't want to go to the bar, don't want to see Vicki and don't want to talk about my brother, but I can't stay in the kitchen all night. "Let's go," I say.

The only difference between the bar and the dining room is that the floor of the bar is covered in linoleum and the dining room with worn green carpet. Tonight the dining room is empty, and the bar isn't much better off. The Shamrock is old, it seems like all we can do to keep it standing sometimes, but what keeps it from being a dive is that most of the customers are old as well. Heavy drinkers, but we don't get meth-heads or violent types. The most violent episode I remember is Hunky asking some woman we'd never seen before to show him her tits. Apparently she was a martial arts expert, or so she said. She went outside, did the splits on the hood of her car, started breathing deeply in and out, punctuating the punches she threw at the air with a Kiiiiya! and yelling for Hunky to come outside so she could kick his fat ass. He locked the door and kept drinking until she left.

I sit down. Vicki notices me right away.

"Jackson," she says, cocking her head and smiling. She stands up, hugs me, squeezes me hard, I'm madly aware of her breasts pressing against me, and kisses my cheek.

"I didn't know you worked here," she says in a southern Missouri twang. "If I'd known I'd of come in before."

"I only work on the weekends." I sit down beside her. Charlie goes to play the juke.

"Let me buy you a beer," she says.

"It's okay. I get a few free."

Hunky lifts his flabby bulldog face. "If a pretty girl wants to buy you a drink you take it, you lazy prick." I will be thirty years old in three months, have been working on and off at the Shamrock since fifteen, and Hunky still calls me a lazy prick every chance he gets. It doesn't matter that he's stopped keeping two dishwashers on the weekends because I can keep up with the dishes myself. I'll pay you an extra two dollars an hour, he'd said. I took it.

"Sure," I say. "I'll take a Miller Lite."

Vicki is still pretty. She's gained some weight, mostly in the hips. There are wrinkles visible even under the makeup, but she still looks better than most girls half her age. At least the ones we get in the Shamrock. We'd go to the drag races when I was a kid, seven or eight. I'd sit on her lap and try to kiss her because it made everyone laugh. He's gonna be a real ladies' man, Vicki said. I never turned into a real ladies' man. I turned into a thirty year old dishwasher.

Trish hands me a beer and Vicki a shot, house whiskey, and a beer to chase it.

"Whiskey?"

"Not often," she says. Suddenly, I'm ten years old and my brother is driving me around the back Cherryville roads, handing me sips of Jack and Coke. It's late, I know that, and I'm not supposed to be out with him but I am. He asks me if I have a girlfriend. I'm a fat kid, I don't point this out, but I tell him no. We're listening to Jim Croce, we listen to that a lot, but not really. Charlie has just played something by AC/DC, who knows what, they all sound the same. Son of a bitch, Hunky says, play some country. I can't stand this thump thump thump bullshit. He slams his fat hand into the bar to punctuate every thump. I don't know where Vicki's man is at. Hunky is on one side of me, a stool between us, and Vicki is on the other side. I have a new beer. Charlie claps me on the shoulder, go play the rest of those songs, he says, I don't know anything about country music. He sits down next to Linda—She's too thin, but Charlie says he likes them that way.

I think about asking Vicki if she wants to go with me, help pick out some songs, but I don't. I'm particular about my drinking music. There are five plays left. I feel Vicki staring at me, burning a hole in my back, as I pick the songs. I realize I might be imagining this, that I probably am. My brother's friend, Eddie, once showed me a Dixie flag. There was something dried and flaky on it. He pointed it out to me. "I've gut a lot of fish on this," he said. It wasn't until years later, once I'd started masturbating, that I finally figured out what the hell he was talking about.

I'm dying, I think. This is too much. I'm going to have a panic attack, so I down my beer in one swallow. I pick songs and tell myself that like every Friday night I'm going to have a few beers and go home to read or play video games. The new Stephen King book is waiting for me, and I have a few comics I've not read yet. My wife will want me home by midnight.

There is another beer waiting for me when I sit back down. My stool is closer to Vicki now I think. We are shoulder to shoulder. Charlie's songs are still playing, Tom Petty, not bad, Hunky isn't even complaining. He's singing along, quietly and badly, to "American Girl," his flabby jowls trembling like blinds in a shallow wind. Charlie has made Linda laugh, it makes her prettier, maybe he'll get lucky. Sometimes he does.

"So," I say.

"So," Vicki says. She sounds cheerful, but if I remember right, she always sounds cheerful.

"Who's that guy that came in with you?" I've made two mistakes. First, I've gotten personal.

"You saw me come in?"

"Yeah, but I had to hurry to the back and finish cleaning up."

"My husband."

I order a whiskey. Trish hesitates, but she brings me one.

"Where is he?" I ask.

"His friend picked him up. They're going to get some stuff."

"Stuff?"

"Stuff," she says.

Charlie's hand is on Linda's bony knee. A good sign for him. He's my only friend —a metal head from St. Louis who moved to the country after leaving his second wife. He works sixty hours a week and most of it goes to child support. I am explaining to Vicki that I am married too. We are living in an apartment. My wife works at the mental hospital. Good benefits. I'm going to school.

"Aren't you too old for school?" I try to imagine her thinking I'm old. Then I remember I'm nine years older than she was when her and Billy were in the automobile accident.

"I can only go half time," I say. "Have to work."

"This isn't the sort of job I pictured you for," she says. "You never did like to get your hands dirty."

"In this job your hands are never dirty long."

"You know what I mean." She wasn't smiling. "You were always the one with the brains. Remember that poem you wrote for me when I was in the hospital? And your Aunt Martha swore you were going to be a preacher. We all thought so."

I'm just going to go home, maybe get a soda and a candy bar on the way, read some comic books or something. The sort of thing I used to do. But Vicki orders us a beer and whiskey. You haven't even heard your songs yet, have you? She wants to know. I tell her I haven't. Good then, she says.

I shouldn't be drinking whiskey. My wife will be upset. She'll show me the scar on her lip, maybe go to her mother's for a few days and take the girl with her. I drink the whiskey anyway. It's cheap, but it doesn't taste like it to me. It tastes like something I've been missing.

"What are you going to school for?"

"The lazy prick has been going to school for as long as I can remember," Hunky says. Charlie tells him to leave me the fuck alone, and he gets away with it because he's a good cook who works cheap and he's a big guy. Even bigger than Hunky, who is over six feet and big bellied. Only his belly and face are fat, his arms and legs are thin and he has no ass. It's like somebody has stuck a plum on a grapefruit then put some toothpicks in it and called it a man. Hunky looks at Charlie for a second, like he's going to say something, then goes back to his beer. Charlie is still hitting up Linda and bobbing his head to something or other by Pantera, I'm not sure what. I'm with Hunky on this one. I can't understand this music.

"Anyway," Vicki says, rolling her eyes, "what are you going to school for?"

"History."

She doesn't even contemplate this. Instead she leans closer, her mouth almost touching my neck, and inhales. "You smell like soap and hamburgers," she says.

"You'd be surprised how many women dig that."

Linda laughs. She's got her hand on Charlie's leg and he's whispering something to her. I imagine he's telling her he has a little pot left and asking if they can go back to her place. Of course, he could be saying something heartbreaking and beautiful.

"Get these bastards a beer," Hunky says, pointing to me and Charlie. Hunky is here every night, usually drunk by this time. There was a period of about a month when he wasn't around much. He would call me down to his trailer, only about 100 yards from the Shamrock, to get money for the bar or to pick up the checks or to ask me to pour bleach into his septic tank. His Chow, sixty pounds overweight and shaved, would start growling at me before I even made it to the portable iron stairs he called a porch. I'd stand out in his dirt yard and yell for him until he opened the door and calmed the dog with a steak bone or a kick in the ribs. This dog ain't going to bite you, he'd say. You chicken shit, he'd say. Then he'd invite me in. He was almost always shirtless and his trailer would be cluttered with empty microwave food containers, gun and cooking magazines, dirty dishes. I finally asked him where the hell he'd been and why he wasn't spending any time at the bar. He said, only reason I ever drank was so I could sleep. Been drinking Nyquil.

Vicki's head is on my shoulder. Her face looks green, but it's from the neon Shamrock above the bar.

"Is she drunk?" Trish asks.

"I don't know," I say.

"I'm not," she says. "I'm tired. Plum worn out."

Finally my songs start. Hank Williams first, "I'm so Lonesome I Could Cry."

"That's music," Hunky says. Charlie rolls his eyes, but I'm pretty sure he really doesn't mind. We always share our jukebox money, and he always plays metal and I always play country. Sometimes I'll throw in Springsteen, CCR or even Jerry Lee, and he'll throw in Tom Petty or Elvis and we get along fine like that.

"You have a daughter?"

"Yeah, Sally."

"How old is she?" Vicki puts her hand on my forearm.

"Eight."

"Does she look like you or the wife?" She's straining to sound cheerful. I could, of course, be seeing something that isn't there. She may actually be interested. She probably is. She's a good girl, I can see that. But then I remember this image, and it's just an image, we're camping. I'm very young. Everyone is sitting around the campfire. It's still daylight, but they are drinking. I wander off. Vicki is behind the camper, arms crossed, she's crying. My brother Billy is on his knees in front of her, begging something of her. I can't hear what. I think now about asking Vicki, but I don't want to know. She might not even remember, probably wouldn't remember, but I've spent many nights wondering. I think, maybe that's when he asked her to marry him but I know that's not true. I can see it clearly and he was asking forgiveness for something. Maybe he'd cheated on her. I don't know.

Vicki pokes me in the ribs. You or the wife, she says again.

"Me," I say.

"Let me see a picture." I pull out my wallet and give the only one I have. It's about a year old.

"She looks like Billy."

Oh Jesus, I think. Jesus Jesus Jesus. I ask for another shot of whiskey, but Trish doesn't give it to me. She gives me a beer instead. You don't drink whiskey, she says, remember. She says that because every time anyone has asked to buy me a shot of whiskey I've turned them down. I don't drink whiskey, I say, and finally any one who comes in there regularly enough to ask has stopped asking.

"You know this boy?" Hunky asks Vicki.

"I wouldn't call him a boy anymore," she says. "But yeah, I do."

"I practically raised this boy." He points a gun-barrel finger at me.

"I know that's not true," Vicki says. It is an exaggeration, of course. But Hunky's own son is in the pen, so I let it slide.

"I've been working here a long time," I say.

"Best dishwasher we've ever had."

"Yeah," Charlie says, "He's the Michael Jordan of dish washing."

I think about all that time in school, how long it's taking. I want to explain this to Vicki. That I write, that I am going to be a teacher, that it really doesn't matter and that I'm never as happy as I am when I'm washing dishes. That if it wasn't for the wife, the kid, that's where I'd stay. It's just not the kind of thing you tell a person though, at least not a person who has some sort of stake, no matter how shallow, in how you turn out.

"You know that night," Vicki says. And I know she's drunk, that she wouldn't be starting off a sentence like that if she wasn't drunk. That, like me, she's probably been spending most of her life trying her best not to start off a sentence like that. Unless she's drunk. And I understand that I'm going to listen to her, although I'd rather not. I'd rather go home. Read. Kiss my girl good night, and lay down next to a wife who will hate me for the next few days.

"It was a good night," she says.

"What?"

"I don't mean the accident, Jackson. I mean the before that." She sounds like a woman who hasn't had many good nights.

"How so?"

"I can't remember. I just know that it was."

"Were you guys drunk," I ask.

"I don't know. I can't remember the accident either. We probably were. I would bet we were."

I nod. I had pieced together enough of what I could remember objectively about my brother to figure that much out. The time he showed me the gun and the Jack bottle in a box under the seat of his truck. The time I was sleeping in the living room where it was cooler in the summer and he came home late, laid down by me and told me about the girl who'd played the "slobbery me blues on his meat horn." All those times he took me up to Abe's and bought me a candy bar and a soda. When some guy pulled into our driveway asking for him, and he walked outside in nothing but his underwear (mostly just the band) and grabbed the guy by the back of his hair and slammed his head over and over into the driver's side window of his car. When we watched Phantasm together and he left the bedroom light on so I could sleep. That he was one week away from marrying this woman who now had her hand on my inner thigh.

"You have the same eyes," she says.

"I know," I say.

"Since I Don't Have You," the original by the Skyliners, blares from the jukebox. I ask Charlie if he played it. I certainly didn't.

"Are you kidding?" he asks.

"I didn't even know that it was on there," I say. "Good tune though."

"Want to dance?" Vicki asks. I think about it. It wouldn't be the first time a few drunks have cut a rug in the Shamrock, but it doesn't happen often either.

"Jackson's going to get him some jaws," Hunky says.

"What's the jaws?"

Charlie laughs.

"Fuck you, Hunky," I say.

"What's the jaws?"

"You don't want to know."

"You know," Hunky says. "The jaws." He moves his hand up and down in front of his mouth—universal blow job sign. I hit him in the face with my beer bottle. It doesn't break like it would in a movie, it's just a thud. Vicki and Linda scream. Trish stands still, mouth open.

"Damn," Charlie says. "Rock on, bro."

Hunky is face down on the bar, mouth open and bleeding. There is a pool of blood on the bar with a tooth in it. I figure his jaw is broke. He's out cold but breathing. The jukebox has stopped.

Vicki's husband walks in. He's thin, there are dark circles under his eyes, bad teeth, he's a tweaker if I ever saw one. He starts walking toward Vicki. Then he assesses the situation. Holy shit, he says. We have got to get the fuck out of here. The front door rattles again. The door knob turns left and right, left and right, until finally whatever is behind it, by trial and error or accident, gets it open. Billy shambles in. His chest is caved in, a rib sticking out above his left tit, and one of his eyes hangs out of its socket. The husband waves to Vicki to come on, but she shakes her head no. Hunky's head is still on the bar, though he's talking.

"You're fired," he says.

"I figured," I say. "Now go home. Get some sleep you fat fuck and learn how to treat people or next time I'll slit your fat turkey neck."

Billy sits down at the bar. "Braaainnnsh," he says. No one pays him any mind. "Braiinnnsh." Finally, Trish hands him a whiskey.

"Damn it, Vicki," the husband says. She finally moves. She leaves the bar with her husband. Billy stays. I look him in his dead eyes. Slowly his feet start to move back and forth, a slow, slow waltz. We dance.

RUBY

Ruby looked like a bulldog. She was on my ass as soon as I walked into the Shamrock. It was 8:30 in the morning and I had a hangover. It hadn't been that long ago that I'd had a nice job up north, but I'd ended up back in my hometown of Cherryville, Missouri, after the divorce.

"Did you work last night?" Of course I had worked. There were only two dishwashers, and I always worked the weekends.

"Yeah," I said. "I worked."

"Well you didn't finish the job, did ya?"

It was the same thing every Sunday morning. I cooked on Sundays because it was slow and no one else wanted to do it. It was ten dollars an hour, while washing dishes was only six, so I couldn't pass it up. The problem was being stuck on an eleven hour shift with Ruby. Ruby hated me. She hated all men, but I was close to the top of her list.

"What do you mean?" I had an idea. I had started drinking early the night before, and was pretty shitty by the time clean up came around.

"No offense," she said, "you left me this pan." She held up a crusty soup pot. "And there's a box back there you didn't take out. This place is a mess."

When wasn't the place a mess? The wall behind the dishwasher was yellow, soft and on the verge of collapse. Our hot water heater wouldn't stay lit for over half an hour at a time, and the grease behind the grill was thick and caked onto the walls.

"Sorry about that," I said, turning on the fryers, then wiping the grease from my hands on my apron.

"No offense," she said. "I'm just saying."

Nothing Ruby said was ever an offense.

Ruby plugged in the radio, 102.5, easy listening. By ten I had made the meat and stuck it in the warmer, finished the biscuits and gravy and had the pancake mix ready to go. It was time to rock and roll. Sunday was the only day of the week we served breakfast—although we didn't actually start until about ten or eleven, whenever we felt like it really. The owner, Hunky, didn't come in on Sundays so we sort of did whatever we wanted. I wanted to start the day out with a shot of Seagram's VO.

"You're not supposed to drink until after we close," Ruby said.

I ignored her, walked behind the bar, poured a shot and took it. I handed Ruby the empty glass. I was dying for a smoke. I'd given them up when my wife left, thinking it might help get my life back in order. It could have been a good start if I'd not imploded and lost my job working for the city a week later. Apparently my foreman didn't like being called a prick. It didn't matter. I'd washed dishes most of my life and didn't mind doing it again. There was a pattern to it anyway, a sort of lullaby. And it paid the child support.

Ruby, probably sensing my desire, lit up—one of those long, brown, old woman cigarettes that smell like fiberglass. The bartender, Bre, walked through the front door, throwing her purse on the bar and started digging through it.

"Hey guys," she said and took some makeup out of her purse. When she was done, she took a Newport from her pack and lit up. I went to the back, sat on a milk crate next to the grill and waited. Waiting had become a significant part of my life. Eventually Ruby found me.

"Can I show you something?" It was a rhetorical

question. She had something to show me every week, nothing fabulous, of course, like Bob Barker might show you. Instead it usually revolved around the same theme— I'd put something in the wrong place.

"See these little baskets," she said, pointing to a pair of green cracker baskets I'd put on a shelf near the heat lamps, where the cooks had asked me to put them.

Ruby and I stared at each other for a second, like mirror images, mimes, until I realized that she actually wanted me to answer her.

"Yeah," I said.

"These go out to the waitress station."

"Charlie asked me to keep a few back here for kid's fries," I said.

"Charlie is an asshole. Charlie hasn't been here long enough to say what goes where." Ruby chewed on the inside of her jaw like it was Juicy Fruit.

"Jon liked a few back here as well." My argument was hopeless. Ruby shrugged it off, feeling no need to explain to me what exactly she thought of Jon. My guess, asshole. He had, after all, been fired for stealing cases of beer. He'd come in Sunday mornings, open the beer cage, grab some Bud Light and stick it in his trunk. We'd all suspected him, but Hunky had gotten the proof when he hid a video camera in the back. Jon had denied it, but when confronted with the proof, shook his head violently, threw his apron in a heap upon the kitchen floor and left.

"If you get lost, just look at the labels. They'll tell you where everything goes. That way, I won't have to come in here and clean up after you every day."

Ruby had, at some point, labeled the entire kitchen, the walk-in cooler, and the stockrooms with masking tape and a Sharpie.

"These are just a few things that are important to me."

I wanted to say, you're a fifty-six year old dishwasher, you look like a truck driver and this is important to you? But I didn't. I wasn't doing so great for myself either.

Bre was a different story all together. There was something familiar about her in a way that was scary to me. She'd stick around most nights and watch me get drunk, although she didn't drink herself. There just wasn't any work in her town, not much anywhere.

"Who's waiting the late shift?" I asked.

Bre exhaled a plume of smoke that crept across the bar. My nic fit kicked into high gear.

"I don't know," she said. "Maybe Angel."

I nodded. Not bad. She worked hard anyway. Even if, as Hunky's sister, she sort of made her own schedule, showing up for work when she felt like it.

The bar was empty, but it still looked cramped. There was just enough room between the wobbly tables to walk. In an attempt to liven the place up, Hunky had commissioned some kid to paint Shamrocks on all the windows, but they were already chipped and covered in dust. Most of the green neon behind the bar had already begun to fade, if not blink out for good. Fridays and Saturdays were still decent nights, but even in Southern Missouri the chains were taking over. Rumor had it they were even going to break ground on an Applebee's across the street.

"Looks like it's going to be another slow one," I said, pulling a crumpled bill out of my wallet for the juke.

"Probably so," she said.

"Any requests?"

"Fly Me to the Moon."

I played it first. It was one of Bre's favorites, but we didn't usually spend a play on it. It wasn't the sort of thing you wanted to crank out for rednecks, so we saved it for slow times or after close.

"Jesus," I said. "Give me another shot then. And a cigarette."

"One more," she said, "and that'll be plenty for this early. No cigs though. You quit, remember?"

Yeah, I remembered. But, I'd quit drinking too. I didn't remind her of that. I downed my shot and went to the back to see if there was anything else I could possibly prep. I ended up giving the gravy a couple of stirs to keep it from scorching and cleaning an already spotless grill.

Ruby was no where to be found. Maybe she'd decided to go home until someone called her to let her know business had picked up. She did sometimes.

I made a sweep of the kitchen and stock rooms to see if there was anything that I could clean. Cleaning was monotonous, brain numbing, right up my alley. The dry goods shelf was full of hard little mouse turds, and I'd been putting off that monster for weeks. It wasn't just the mouse shit. It was the cans, the bags, the six oz. juices—hundreds of things I'd have to take off the shelf, find someplace to put and then replace once every thing was clean. It'd take hours.

Hunky had asked Ruby to do it, but she'd told him that she busted her ass around the place and wasn't about to do anything extra until someone else got off their ass and did something.

I was filling up a bucket with bleach water and about to get down to it when Bre called out the morning's first order. A few eggs over easy, sausage and a short stack. I whipped it out in a few minutes, figured I'd done enough work, and made my way back to the bar. I was a little buzzed, thirsty as hell, but I knew there wasn't any chance of getting another shot just yet. Bre could be stubborn about that sort of thing. I poured a Diet Coke instead.

Joseph was sitting at a small, two-top table near the juke. Most Sundays he opened and closed the place. He was a Wild Turkey and water man. He gave me a wave and a thumbs up, shoveling pancakes into his mouth. He was a pretty suave guy for an older dude—gray hair oiled back, pearl snaps on a neatly pressed shirt, clean fingernails. Bre was sitting with him, smiling about something or other, twirling a strand of hair around her finger.

I had a chance to grab another shot. No one would have noticed, but the shitty ass truth of the matter was, I didn't need another one. Bre knew what she was talking about. One more and I wouldn't be able to stop myself from blacking out.

The bell above the door rang. A big group walked in.

"And another angel gets its wings," Joseph said.

I was sweating my ass off in the kitchen. An order would be coming. The bell rang again. Then again. What the fuck? I swung open the beaten up door that separated the kitchen and the dining room; we were packed. Four big tables. Joseph gave me a smile and a wave, took a swig of his Wild Turkey, and chuckled.

"Order," Bre said, and before I had it down she was yelling out another one. Jesus Christ, one of the reasons I only cooked on Sunday's was because I just wasn't that good at it, and I'd never had orders like this before. I couldn't keep up. I sent out an omelet with no cheese.

"No offense, but you don't look like you're doing too good."

Where the hell did Ruby come from? I swear to

God, sometimes it was like she had radar. If something turned up missing, Ruby always knew where to find it. Looking for to go cups, ask Ruby. Tongs missing, Ruby She hid things just so she would be the only one who knew where they were at.

"Can you throw on some hash browns?" I asked. Ruby did.

The rush wasn't ending. Bre was about to pull her hair out, but Angel was supposedly on her way. I was so far behind, even with Ruby's limited help, that I was throwing orders at the grill randomly.

"I called Charlie." Bre handed me another order. "He's on his way."

"Thank God," I said. The rush wouldn't faze him.

I was deep in the dregs by the time he arrived. I'd pretty much just given up—a small table had already walked out—a cardinal sin in the restaurant business. Charlie surveyed the damaged through glassy eyes, smiled a bit, lit up a joint right in the kitchen and got to work. I was moved to the fryers, dropping whatever he yelled out to me into a vat of bubbling grease.

"What's that smell?" Ruby said.

"It's nothing."

"Something stinks back here."

"I can't smell a thing? You smell anything, Jackson?"

"I just dropped a catfish," I said.

"Fuck you guys," Ruby snorted. "No offense, but fuck you both. It smells like grass back here."

"Grass?" Charlie asked.

"Weed." If there was anyone Ruby hated more than me, it was Charlie.

"Never heard of it," he said, taking a break just long enough to stick a fingerprint covered Ozzie CD into the player.

"Oh no," Ruby said. "I ain't gonna listen to that shit."

"I'm not busting out this mess listening to elevator music," Charlie said and threw a hamburger onto the grill where it popped and sputtered.

It didn't take long for Charlie to get things under control, and when he did, we stepped into the bar area where it was cooler. Joseph was nursing another drink.

"Give me a Jack and Coke," Charlie said.

"You can't drink this early," Ruby reminded him.

"Fuck that noise. I'm not even supposed to be here today."

"You're going to have to start paying on your tab," Bre said, pouring a generous helping of Jack into a rock glass.

"What? Hunky takes fifty dollars a week out of my check just for that."

Bre handed him his drink. Her wedding band caught the light.

"Yeah well, I added it up and you still owe over two hundred dollars."

"Holy shit," I said. "No wonder you can't pay your rent."

"Fuck it," Charlie said. "That's why I work here. Half-priced drinks are better than health insurance."

Ruby grabbed a tub of dishes and marched off. Sometime during the rush, Ron the lush had snuck in. He was already sloppy drunk.

"Play some country, Joseph," he said. "David Allan Coe or something like that."

Joseph nodded. Bre flipped through People—one of their seemingly bi-monthly weight loss issues.

"I always thought she was pretty," Bre flipped another page.

"Who's that?" I asked, pretty women being one of the few things that still piqued my interest.

"Janet Jackson. She's lost a lot of weight again."

"Boy, I wouldn't fuck that for all the gold in Fort Knox," Ron said.

"Jesus," I said, "You're good country people. Ron, you really are. Gimme another drink, darlin.'"

"You OK, Jackson?" Bre looked up from her magazine. She looked concerned, or I was imagining it, it was getting harder to tell.

"I'm fine. I sweated my buzz off back in that hell hole of a kitchen. I'll switch to beer though."

Charlie nudged me as Bre bent over to grab my Miller Lite.

"No offense," Ruby yelled from the back. "But you put this pan in the sink. I told you to put them on the floor and I'd take care of them."

I took a swig of beer. I listened to the juke. I listened to the rattle talk of dirty dishes from the back. I don't know where my mind had wandered off to. I honestly couldn't remember, but according to the clock about fifteen minutes of my life had just passed and I couldn't remember a goddamned second of it.

Charlie was gone, probably home now that the rush was over, and Bre was sitting with Joseph.

Ron leaned close to me.

"You ever fucked one?" he asked.

"Fucked one what, Ron?"

"A black girl," he said.

"Fuck, Ron, go home."

"I'm serious man," he took off his John Deere hat and wiped beads of sweat off his forehead.

I threw my empty bottle into the trash and stared at my tired face in the mirrored wall behind the bar. There was no getting around it, I looked old.

"Well," Ron said, "have ya?" His seemed so eager, I half expected him to whip out his chubby and rub one out right there.

"I'm serious, Ron. Go the fuck home."

"Just tell me, partner. We're buddies, right? We're old pals."

"Bre," I yelled across the bar.

"Aww fuck," Ron said.

"What?'" Bre asked. I jabbed my thumb at Ron and rolled my eyes.

"Time to go, Ron. You're cut off."

"I ain't drunk. I ain't even close to being drunk."

"Now," she said, and made to stand up.

"Aww shucks!" Ron stood up, wobbled, nearly fell, and left.

Ruby yelled from the back. "Goddamn you, Charlie."

Bre and I rushed to the kitchen. Ruby had a pair of scissors cocked around the electrical chord of the CD player.

"I told you I ain't listening to anymore of that shit." Ruby's face was red.

"It's Pantera," Charlie said.

"It's shit." Ruby stomped the floor in her anger, but she stomped right into a small puddle of water, lost her footing, and landed on her ass with a thud. Charlie laughed.

"Fuck you, you piece of shit. You white trash." Ruby's said.

"You've been back here listening to golden oldies for two hours now," Charlie said. "It's my turn."

"The hell it is. I control the radio around here." Ruby made her way back to her feet. "If you play any more of that crap, I'll cut this cord right in two. I swear to God I will."

"What the hell is going on?" Bre asked.

"Charlie turned it off my Nat King Cole CD and put this shit back in."

"Hunky told you that you need to share the CD player, Ruby."

"It's not even his fuckin' day to work."

"Well, he had to come in. We got busy." Both Bre and Ruby looked at me, as if I were the tie-breaking voted. I shrugged.

"He can go home. We're slow now," Ruby said.

"You want to clock out, Jackson?" Charlie asked.

"Hell yeah," I said.

Ruby cut the cord.

I was feeling pretty damn good by closing time. Angel had never made it in and Bre was pretty beat. There wasn't much of a supper rush, nothing I had to help Charlie with. I just drank.

Only me, Charlie, Bre and Ruby were left. Ruby didn't drink, but she had a few more dishes to take care of, and she needed to re-mop the floor. Charlie, as she had put it, "made a goddamned mess of the place."

"I'm out of here, dudes." Charlie downed the last of his whiskey and Coke.

"Already?"

"Yeah, my daughter's coming over tomorrow. I don't wanna be too hung over."

"That's cool," I said. "I guess I'll see you on Wednesday."

"Take care, brother."

"Come over here and have a seat," I said to Bre after I heard the back door shut. "Bring me another beer too. Please."

"I think I'm going to save up for a boob job," she said, tossing her People into the trash, where it landed like a dead bird.

"What for?"

"I don't know. Why not? Why not have great tits?"

"You have great tits."

"I mean perfect tits. God, I'd love to have perfect tits."

"What's your husband think?"

"He's all for it." She pressed her breasts together, looked down at them and sighed.

"I'm playing the juke box." I said.

"Fly me to the moon."

The song started to play, and Frank's voice drifted across the empty bar. The back door slammed shut.

"Ruby must be on her way out," Bre said.

"By the sound of things, she wasn't happy either."

"It was a late night for her. Busy. She's not used to that." We heard pots and pans crashing to the floor in the kitchen.

"What the hell?"

"Did she lock the back door?" Before I could answer Ruby came screaming into the bar, a man in a black ski mask followed close behind her.

"Give me all your money." The man poked the barrel of his gun toward the cash register. He sounded just like a James Cagney.

"What the fuck you laughing at?" He turned to me. There was something familiar about his eyes. Something haunting. I was staring down a barrel. It felt just like I'd always thought it would.

I put up my hands. I'd like to say that at that moment, a gun in my face, I had gotten some sort of perspective on my life. That maybe it flashed in front of my eyes, or some epiphany made it clear where I'd went wrong. I had been a good kid, after all. But I can't. All I could do was wait for that curled finger to twitch.

"Yeah, you better not fucking laugh, smart guy."

Bre stopped pulling money out of the register. She was no longer looking at the man in the mask, but beyond him. A click. "Drop that gun, son."

There stood Ron, a bit wobbly, but steady enough to hold a shotgun.

"Jesus Christ," Ruby said. "Am I glad to see you. No offense."

"I was just takin' me a little nap in my truck when I saw this son of a bitch sneaking around. Took me a minute to wake up and load my gun." He shuffled his feet, embarrassed at being caught off guard with empty rifle.

The man in the mask dropped his pistol. He was trembling. Jesus, he said. Jesus, Jesus, Jesus.

"Jesus ain't gonna help you if you don't take off that mask, boy."

"Look, I just want to get out of here. Please, mister, I want to get out of here."

I really think Ron would have shot him. But Bre was a step ahead of everybody.

"Jon?" She asked. "Jon, is that you?"

"No."

"Yeah, it is. Come on, take the mask off."

"I ain't Jon."

"You're not fooling anybody," I said. "Same height. Same voice. Same weird walk."

"I do not have a weird walk." Reluctantly, he removed the ski mask, his blonde hair tussled and boyish. With a shy grin, he picked up the gun and stuck it in his pocket.

"It ain't loaded," he said.

"Jon." Ron lowered his gun. "I'll be a son of a bitch.

"What the hell are you doing?" Ruby asked.

"I can't pay the rent," he said. "I can't even afford fucking diapers. We're gonna get kicked out. Just give me enough for the rent," he said. "Three hundred dollars."

"You know I can't do that," Bre said.

"Yeah you can. Just tell Hunky you got robbed."

"He'll call the cops," Ruby said. "He'll probably call them anyway."

"We're not going to tell him about this, Ruby." I said. "Jon, here's twenty dollars. It's all I have on me right now. It'll get diapers anyway. Sit down and have a beer. I'll put it on my tab. You want one, Ruby?"

"Why not," she said. "Fuck it."

"This is the first beer I've had since my old man died." Ruby took a swig like she meant it too, like a Viking.

"What happened?" I expected the usual—cancer or heart attack.

"He shot himself after he killed our daughter driving her home from school drunk."

We sat there, drank in silence, and tried not to look at each other.

RUBY RUBY

I came in at 8:20 to prep, and as soon as I walked through the back door Ruby was on my ass. At 34, I was working at The Shamrock again. I had put myself through college as a dishwasher, gone on to teaching composition at a decent university up north, and then lost it all. So when my wife took the kid back to our hometown of Cherry, MO, I followed her.

Without references, I couldn't find a job as an adjunct, so I called my friend Bones and asked if he could put me back on dishes. "Sure thing, Jackson," he said. "A kid just quit."

We served breakfast at the Shamrock, but only on Sundays. Conway didn't want to do it because he didn't wake up that early. I volunteered because it's ten dollars an hour and dishes are only six. We were more bar than grill, although we did a steady food business. We didn't do much for Sunday, especially breakfast, but Bones insisted we keep trying. "It'll catch on," he said. I had my doubts. Sunday mornings are great for most restaurants. They get a big before and after church crowd. But we weren't an after church kind of place.

Ruby was the other dishwasher and I only worked with her on Sundays. I was hung over and her voice was loud.

"Did you work last night?" Ruby asked. Ruby is old. She's was missing her teeth and had a chin full of silver whiskers.

"You know I did, Ruby." My head was pounding. I pulled a lint covered Tylenol out of my front pocket, blew on it, and popped it in my mouth. I chewed it up and swallowed it with coffee. They work faster that way.

"The place is a mess," she said. She was right. I had started drinking early the night before and had left a lot of work behind. Still, I'd heard this spiel so often it was hard to feel ashamed yet again.

"You left me this soup pan," she said, holding it up. The lip was caked black with burnt cheesy potato soup.

"I had to soak it," I said. "I was going to get to it this morning."

"I'll clean it." Ruby grabbed a Tootsie Roll from a bag she religiously kept on top of the dishwasher because the heat helped soften them up. She still couldn't chew them though. She sucked on them like Starlight mints. She didn't do it quietly either.

"You didn't take out the boxes."

"I'll get them," I said.

"I already did." Ruby put on a pair of blue dish-washing gloves and grabbed a new scour from the shelf above the sink. She went through them like mad, because she wouldn't used the same one two days in a row. Germs, she said.

I wanted to make some sort of gesture. I walked around the heat lamps to the sink. The wall behind the dishwasher was soft and yellow. It wouldn't last much longer, but Bones said he didn't have the money to get it fixed. I rooted Ruby out of the way, turned on the faucet—we didn't have a sprayer—and the water was cold. The hot water heater had gone out again.

Ruby placed her gloved hand on my forearm. The glove was cold, and she pushed my arm away from the sink.

"I'll do it," she said. "When you wash dishes this is your station, but when I'm here it's my space, you know. I'll take care of it. You go get ready for breakfast."

After I returned to the grill, Ruby plugged in the radio Bones had brought in after buying himself a new one. It was caked in grease, but it worked, and Ruby tuned it to KEZK, easy listening. Not my type of music, but my aching head appreciated it.

"I am sorry, Ruby." I turned the deep fryers up to 350° and wiped the resultant grease from my fingers onto my apron. Then, I fired up the charbroiler. The flames underneath licked the top grates and the burnt fat caking them began to drip and sizzle.

"I was just saying. You have to think about things." Ruby said. But, I wasn't thinking. I was watching the flames dance. My hangover was fierce and my head felt like it had a hole in it.

By ten I had made all the breakfast meat, stuck it in the warmer, finished the biscuits and gravy and had the pancake mix ready to go. I always made what Bones asked for, even though I ended up throwing most of it away at three. There was nothing left to do but wait. Bre, the bartender, wasn't in yet and we wouldn't open until she was. Ruby was still working on the soup pan I'd left her, so I figured I could grab a free drink before everything got started.

The only thing that separates the kitchen from the bar and dining room is a beat up green door with a small, dingy window to make sure you don't hit anyone coming in or out. As you step through the door, the waitress station is just to the right and the bar is just to the left. I took a left.

It was early, but I had to do something about my head. My shoes stuck to the tile floor as I stepped behind the bar and poured myself a shot of Old Crow, our house whiskey.

"You're not supposed to drink until after close," Ruby said. I'd not heard her come out of the kitchen. She was still sucking on her Tootsie Roll and her mouth moved furiously.

"You're like The Shadow," I said, and took my shot. "You always know." I poured another two fingers, toasted Ruby and downed it.

"You don't have to be an asshole," she said.

"I'm just hung over." I handed Ruby the empty and she stared at it with disinterest.

"You're hung over every Sunday," she said and turned back to the kitchen in a hurry. She can't stand dirty dishes. She can't just let one sit.

I was starting to feel better. I sat at the bar on a wobbly green stool. The Shamrock is pretty depressing when it's empty. The tables are Formica. Half of the chairs are pastel green and the other half are pine—most of them have rips in the vinyl. For some reason known only to him, Hunky—the last owner, carpeted the floor with a deep red plush. The waitresses hated it; they couldn't keep it clean.

The bar ashtrays were full of butts. Ruby wouldn't touch those; it was the bartender's job. After two shots, I was dying for a smoke and I came close to having one. But I had given them up when my wife took our daughter back home. I figured it would be the first step in getting my life back in order. To quit smoking, I'd have to quit drinking. It would, I thought, be something my wife could hold onto.

But a week after quitting, I showed up to an eight o'clock Comp. II with an X carved into my face. I'd carved it there with a steak knife during a black out. It wasn't a deep cut, and I had cut up my arms as well. Calling out of work never even occurred to me.

I started class out with a lecture on wordiness. I could hear a few of the girls in class crying, but it was faint, like a woman sobbing into a pillow. One of the football players asked me if I was okay. I told him he needed to take notes. Then I started shaking and I couldn't stop. I was put in a hospital for a few days after that. They couldn't keep me any longer than two days, because I no longer appeared to be a threat to myself or anyone else. The school was actually decent about it. They offered to pay for rehab, and I refused. Not even tenure could save me then.

So I moved in with my mother back in Cherryville. It was only a five minute drive from where my wife and daughter were staying, but I hadn't yet seen them. It didn't matter. I would eventually. In the mean time, I washed dishes. I had done it most of my life. There was a pattern to it, a sort of lullaby. It was stable. I made a little money, my mom paid all the bills, and I could send my wife flowers every time I got a check. She had always loved flowers and I had always considered them a waste of money. But it was another way to convince her I had changed.

As much as I loved dish washing, I hated cooking. Cooking confused me and made me nervous. It was always hot and there was just so much to keep up with. Bones wouldn't have let me, nor would I have wanted to, do it any day other than Sunday.

The green door opened with a bang. Ruby had her hand closed in a tight fist. She sat down beside me and lit up one of those long brown old lady cigarettes. It smelled like fiberglass. She sat there for a minute without saying anything. Then she slid her cupped, fat hand across the bar toward me. For a minute, I thought she was actually going to hold my hand. Instead, she slowly lifted hers from the bar, like she was doing a trick, and revealed the cleaned shot glass. "You'll probably need this again," she said.

We heard Bre come in the back door.

"I'm going to the back, Ruby," I said. "Looks like it's time to rock and roll."

"I'll believe it when I see it," she said.

Bre was in the kitchen looking things over. She was pretty much the boss when Bones wasn't around. Her brown hair hung just past her shoulders. She wore a button up Cardinal's jersey and faded jeans about a size too tight. By Vogue standards she'd be considered chunky. But I don't read Vogue and I was in love with her. I didn't love her as much as I loved my wife, but it was getting there.

"Hey," I said. My apron was hanging loose around my hips, so I untied it, wrapped the strings around my waist and tried again, but I was having some trouble.

"Jesus, Jackson," Bre said. "Let me get that for you."

I'd gotten pretty thin and she had to wrap the strings twice around my waist. She tied them into a tight knot in the back. "There," she said. "Now can I open this place up?"

By 11:30 we still hadn't had a customer. I was sitting on an orange milk crate in the back near the grill rereading God Bless You, Mr. Rosewater. I had probably read it a hundred times. I hadn't done much work, but I was sweating like I had. Bones hadn't gotten around to putting in the air conditioner he'd promised us. It was cooler at the bar, but I had a jones for another drink and figured I'd better wait it out alone.

It wasn't long until Ruby found me though.

"Can I show you something?" Her eyes were pieces of coal, and she narrowed them at me like she always did when she was about to lecture. "See these little baskets," she said, pointing to a pair of green cracker baskets I'd put on a shelf near the heat lamps. We stared at each other for a minute, mirror images, mimes, until I realized it wasn't a rhetorical question.

"Yeah," I said.

"These go out to the waitress station."

"I know that most of them do," I said. "But Conway likes to keep a few back here to use when we get orders for kid's fries."

"They go out to the waitress station. If Conway needs one, he can walk out there and get it."

"Fine," I said. "It doesn't really make a difference to me either way."

"Look, I'm not trying to be an asshole, Jackson. But these things are important. If you get lost, just look at the labels. They'll tell you where everything goes and I won't have to come in here and clean up after you."

Ruby had, at some point, labeled the entire kitchen, the walk-in cooler, and the stockroom with masking tape and a Sharpie. Her handwriting was meticulous.

"Just try harder," she said.

At noon there still hadn't been an order. My hands were shaking. I had a picture of my daughter in my wallet. Sometimes I would take it out and look at it, but never when I had the shakes. So, I sat down at the bar, took the shot glass out of my apron, and handed it to Bre. She filled it, gave it back to me and squeezed my hand. "Try to take it easy," she said. "It's still early." I nodded.

"Who's working the late shift?" I asked.

Bre lit up a cigarette and exhaled a plume of smoke that rekindled my nic fit. "Angel," she said. "If she decides to show up." Angel is Bones' twin sister. She shows up when she feels like it, mostly just to help out. Her husband is the principal at Cherryville High, so she doesn't exactly need the money.

"We'll be slow though," Bre said. "I can handle it without her. In the mean time, Bones wants us to hang up these things."

Bre pulled a stack of shiny green foil shamrocks from a chipped shelf behind the bar. They were about the size of a human head and strung together with fishing line.

"They're tacky," I said. The look of them made me queasy.

"He thinks they'll liven the place up."

"You go ahead, I'm playing the juke."

"Whatever, Jackson." She started digging for tape in the drawer underneath the cash register. "You'd just fuck it up anyway."

That's the sort of thing people say without thinking. It's the sort of thing that can really bother a person if they let it.

The only decent thing we had at The Shamrock was one of those new digital jukeboxes. You could download anything on it. I played "Fly Me to the Moon" first—it was one of Bre's favorites. I followed it with Robert Johnson's "Crossroads." I hate the Clapton version; it doesn't have any soul.

When I was done, I sat at the bar and watched Bre finish the decorations. The gaudy shamrocks hung in reverse arcs and reflected the neon from all the beer signs. The dining room and bar were kaleidoscopes. Light bounced everywhere.

"It looks like hell," I said. "It's a redneck disco."

"I did the best I could." Bre sat beside me. She sipped on a Sprite. Her lips were full and heart shaped. My wife's had been as well.

"Can I have another shot?" I asked.

"One more," she said. As she stood up I caught

a flash of skin; she tugged at her jersey, pulling it to her waist. I reached for the pack of Newports she'd left on the bar.

"No cigarettes," she said. "You quit, remember. Now drink your shot and get back to the kitchen and clean something. I can't stand to watch you listen to that depressing shit you play on the jukebox and drink all day."

The kitchen was empty. Ruby had probably gone home for a bit. She sometimes did when it was slow. Bre would call her when things picked up. I made a sweep of the place. Cleaning was monotonous, brain numbing, but I had to do something. The dry goods shelf was full of hard little rat turds. I had put off cleaning it for weeks, but Ruby had taken care of everything else and Bones had asked me to do it several times.

I found a pair of rubber gloves, filled a bucket with bleach water and took down the cans and powdered mixes from the shelf. It stunk. Rat turds the size of raisins mixed in with dried cornmeal and covered in a layer of grease. I dipped a wire mesh scour in the bleach water and began to scrub. I worked from the top down, sweat running into my eyes, scrubbing until the muscles in my right arm burned and felt like rubber.

I found a half-dead black rat in one of the Victor traps Bones had set out. One eye popped out of its socket and hung on by a fiber of optic nerve. Its back was broken and around the iron bar of the trap, its belly distended and heaved rapidly. I nearly retched and shoved a 42 ounce can of Cantida Tomato sauce in front of it. Someone else would have to take care of it.

"I brought you something," Ruby said. I jumped and banged my head on the bottom lip of the second shelf.

"You scared the shit out of me, Ruby." I rubbed the crown of my head. There was a small bump, but no blood.

"Look," Ruby said. She pinched a clover between her stubby forefinger and thumb. "It's only a three leaf. I've been outside looking for shamrocks, but I can only find three leafs."

I didn't know what to say to that.

"This one is for you," she said. "But let me get some tape first. If we put scotch tape over it, it'll last."

"You do that, Ruby," I said. The shelf wasn't totally done, but I'd had enough. I put the stock back where Ruby's labels said it should go. Then, I scrubbed my hands under the sink with bleach water until they were red.

I was drenched in sweat. I'd had enough of the kitchen and went back to the bar. Charlie, one of the regulars, sat at the table near the juke sipping a Wild Turkey on the Rocks. Bre sat across from him twirling a lock of hair around her finger. My wife had done that on our first date. It had driven me wild and I fell in love with her that night, long before she had fallen in love with me.

Charlie opened and closed the place on Sundays. He was a loyal Wild Turkey man. I don't know how drunk it got him. He sipped. I never talked to him—didn't want to talk to him. I felt too sorry for him to talk to him. He wore the same thing every Sunday, a red crushed velvet smoking jacket like he was Hugh Hefner, a pair of pressed black slacks and a white shirt with pearl snaps. His hair was gray and he kept it slicked back with pomade in a pompadour. It broke my heart.

Charlie gave me a nod as I stepped behind the bar to pour my own drink. Bre turned briefly, but said nothing. Charlie spread his dry lips in a smile and held his empty glass up to me. I toasted him and took my shot. I felt dizzy. I couldn't get the rat, the way it heaved its last breaths, out of my head. Back broken, trying to breathe when you can't; it's not a good way to die.

Charlie still held his drink up and stared at me with watery eyes. His fingernails were long and yellow.

I think he wanted me to refill it for him. He clinked his wedding ring against the side of the glass three times, rapidly. I'd never seen his wife. She was probably dead. He wouldn't set the glass down and I couldn't stop looking at it. White dots floated in front of my eyes; my blood pressure was up. Bre glared at me before taking the glass from Charlie.

She was refilling the drink when a red SUV pulled into the lot near the front door. From the bar, you can see the entire parking lot. It's gravel, Bones won't pave it, and just beyond that, on the other side of the road, is an abandoned, overgrown field, and even farther Cherryville graveyard. It can only be seen in the winter when the weeds and trees in the field have died.

A group of eight got out of the SUV and walked in, chit-chatting, laughing. A family, you could tell—they all had the same pinched faces and wispy hair. I was still behind the bar with Bre thinking about another shot.

"Bre," I said. "Call Conway. I'm done for the day."

"What?" She sat Charlie's drink on the bar. It slid a little to the left.

"Look," I said. "I'm done."

"Jesus fucking Christ," she said and picked up the house phone. The customers sat themselves at the big table. I hated to have Bre call Conway in, but I just didn't know what else to do.

"Bones is going to kill you," Bre said. "But Conway will be here in five minutes." She picked up Charlie's drink, took it to him, and he toasted me again. Then she pulled a white Bic and a waitress pad from her apron and walked over to table and began taking orders.

Bre glanced at me as I quickly made my way to the men's restroom. I had to push my foot against the bottom of the door to get the bolt lock close enough to the hole that had been drilled into the jamb for it. I turned on the cold water and splashed my face with it. It didn't help. I puked until there was nothing left but dry heaves. My eyes felt like blood ticks. I was pale and I couldn't stop shaking. I splashed some more water on my face; the toilet smelled acrid. I flushed it. Customers scurried outside the bathroom door.

Someone knocked. "Occupied," I said, but they knocked again.

"Someone is in here."

They knocked again. It was insistent. I opened the door.

Ruby handed me a three leaf clover pressed in tape.

"Conway wants to know if you can help him out for just a few minutes," she said.

Conway was throwing some food on the grill, so I took the fryers. Drop some catfish he said, and as many fries as you can fit in. The flat grill sizzled with burgers—blood and grease popped. My stomach rumbled, but I got a hold of myself and began to work. I was messing everything up though.

"Hold up," Conway said. "Just stop everything for a second. Don't move."

I held a raw chicken breast in my hand that I had been about to roll in flour.

"Listen," Conway said. He pulled a joint from his front pocket and lit it. "We're going to bust this shit out. Just relax." He sat his spatula down, took a hit off the joint, and changed the radio station to KSHE 95—"War Pigs" had just started.

I shook my head when Conway offered me a hit off the joint. He shrugged his broad shoulders and began to cook. He had the grill clear in about twenty minutes and was ready for a drink.

Conway and I sat at the bar. The customers were fed, looked happy, and would leave soon. Conway ordered a Jack and Coke. He was bald and wore a plain black bandanna Hulk Hogan style. He took it off, wadded it up, and wiped his face with it before shoving it into his front pocket. Ruby marched back and forth between the kitchen and the dining room, the green door swinging wildly, taking only one or two dishes back with her at a time.

"I have my daughter with me this weekend, Jackson," Conway said. "Lucky for you, I need the extra money."

"I'm sorry," I said. "I guess I sort of freaked out there."

"These bitches need to stop giving you drinks," he said. "I don't know why the fuck they do it. I don't know why Bones let's them do it. I know he's your buddy, but shit. It's about time you got a hold on yourself."

"At least he pays," Bre said. "You still owe two hundred on your tab."

Conway shook the last drink of whiskey and Coke into his mouth. "Fuck it," he said. "It's no big deal, Jackson. Like I said, I need the money."

Ruby kicked the door back open. The customers were shuffling out. She picked up a bus tub and started clearing off an empty table.

"Do you want me to get that," I said.

"You're off the clock, Jackson. I'll get it."

Bre handed me a cold Miller Lite. "You're switching to beer," she said. She fixed Conway another drink on the house and sat down between us. She smelled like White Diamonds. I had bought my wife a bottle of it our last anniversary. I didn't want to think about that at work. It would just lead to a lot of stuff I didn't want to think about at work.

I couldn't think of anything to say to either one of them. We sat there for a bit, until a beat up, Ford truck slid into the parking lot at an angle, kicked up gravel and barely stopped before hitting the front door. The truck was hunter green, but the hood was dull red primer.

"Shit," Bre said.

It was Ron. He came in two or three times a week and drank until he couldn't walk. Charlie, still sitting in the corner nursing a Turkey on the rocks, chuckled.

"How yawl doin'?" Ron said as he stumbled through the door.

"Don't serve him," I said, putting my hand on Bre's thigh and squeezing for emphasis. It felt strange and familiar. She stood up.

"Bones says to," she said. "At least until he gives us a reason."

Ron's face was red and bloated. "Play some country," he said. "David Allan Coe." He threw a five dollar bill at me. I played the music. When I got back, Ron was sitting by Bre and he had a Budweiser in front of him. Bre flipped listlessly through a copy of People. Janet Jackson was on the cover. She'd lost 40 pounds again, and Bre was reading all about it.

"She's pretty," I said. Bre nodded and closed the magazine.

"I wouldn't fuck it for all the gold in Fort Knox," Ron said, finishing his beer and pushing the empty bottle toward Bre.

"I'm sure she'll be sorry to hear that, Ron." Bre said and walked around to the other side of the bar. "I might as well stay back here now."

I took a drink and listened to the rattle of dirty dishes coming from the kitchen. My mind wandered off after that. It's a bad sign. It means a blackout is coming. When I looked back up at the clock a half an hour had passed that I couldn't remember.

Conway was gone, probably doing something in the kitchen. Ron was working on a beer next to me. Bre sat across from Charlie again, laughing at something. I watched her for a bit. She was good to me. She stayed with me at night and let me drink until I could barely stand. I don't drive anymore, and usually walked to work, but she always drove me home. We'd talk about a lot of things on the way, most of which I never remembered the next day. I know that her husband had cheated on her. He coached the girl's basketball team and had slept with one of the seniors. He'd been fired for it, there had been a scandal, but Bre had taken him back. Still, she may as well have been a stranger. Like I said, I was in love with her, but that didn't change things.

.

Ron propped his forearm on the bar and leaned in close to me.

"You fuck around on your wife," he asked. His pasty jowls trembled as he talked.

Bre sat with Charlie, her chin resting in the palm of her hand. She was apparently fascinated.

"Ron don't start or I'll have you kicked out." I said. I knew where he was going. I'd heard it my entire life from one Ron or another and this one started it every time he had too many. When I graduated I thought that I'd gotten away from it. I'd moved. I had a good job. My wife loved me. The town we lived it was clean. But my drinking had gotten the best of me and I'd ended up right back where I started.

"You don't fuck around?" Ron tossed the copy of People at me. It nearly hit me in the face before I fended it off. Ron took his hat off and wiped beads of sweat off of his forehead with the back of his hand. I threw my empty bottle into the trash where it clanked around with the others like rattling bones in a horror house. Ron nudged me with his elbow. It was like falling into a side of raw meat.

"Leave," I said. "You know Bones don't let people talk like that in here."

"I ain't fucking going nowhere until you tell me." His breath smelled like stale beer and buffalo wings.

"I'm serious, Ron. Go home."

"Tell me partner. You know me. We're buddies, right. Old pals." His voice was a near whisper. "Yeah, we're old buddies. I know you fuck around."

I put my hands to my face, my thumbs just under my cheek bones, my fingers pressing at my temples. "I don't know you," I said. "We're not friends."

"Sure we are." Ron belched. It stank like meat.

"Bre. Bre." Jesus, I was screaming. Another anxiety attack.

Bre stood up and clasped her hands in front of her face, fingertips pressed to her pursed lips like a prayer.

"Ron," Bre said. "Go home." She pressed her fingers together so tightly they turned white.

"I'm not drunk," Ron said. "I ain't even close to being drunk and Bones says I can stay here until I am drunk."

"Bones doesn't come in on Sundays," Bre said. "I do." She rolled her eyes at me, as if it was all somehow my fault.

"I was just fucking with the boy," Ron said. "It was all in fun."

"It's not fun," I said. I grabbed him by the collar and clenched my fists. "It's not by God fun."

"Stop it!" Bre said. "Get the fuck out of here, Ron."

It wasn't easy because he's so big, but I pulled Ron into me by the collar of his flannel shirt. I wanted to kill him. He did this shit to me every Sunday because he knew it got under my skin.

"You don't know anything about me," I said. Our faces were nearly touching. "Not a goddamned thing. You hear me you redneck piece of shit?"

Ron smiled. One of his incisors was black and chipped.

"I know all about it," Ron said and his breath made my stomach turn again. I let him go.

"See you later," he said.

Ron did three donuts in the parking lot before speeding off. A rock shot out from one of the back tires and struck a window. It didn't break.

"I'm sorry," Bre said and handed me a shot. It was something dark and rich. It tasted sweet and I drank them until Bre locked the front door. It was still early, but we hadn't had any more customers. Conway left right away. He had to pick his daughter up from his sister and then take her back to her mom. Ruby still had the kitchen to clean. She would have to sweep, mop, take out the trash.

The shots, whatever they were, went to my head. I'd feel it the next morning. I asked for a beer. There was frost on the bottle of Miller Lite. I rubbed it against my forehead.

"Come over here and have a seat," I said, patting the stool next to me.

"Let me add up the tickets first," Bre laid them out

in front of her. There weren't many. "Play something. I'll be done in a minute."

I put two dollars in the juke. It was all the cash I had left. I only got four songs out of it. The digital jukes are nice, but they're expensive. I played "Ode to Billy Jo" first. Bobbie Gentry's smooth voice filled the empty room.

By the time I picked the other three songs, Bre was done with the tickets and sitting at the customer side of the bar. She was drinking a Mojito.

"How long we going to be here tonight, Jackson?" I could smell the mint on her breath.

"Not long," I said. "We'll wait for Ruby and go."

"I'm going to have to start cutting you off," she said.

"You know you can't do that." The foil shamrocks looked dull now that Bre had turned down the lights.

"It's for your own good," she said. "I know. Your wife. Your daughter. Bones says it's okay. He's your buddy. I realize that. I can't do it. I won't do it anymore."

The neon green shamrock sign behind the bar cast a pale glow upon us. The last haunting chord of "Ode to Billie Joe" echoed across the bar and Sinatra began to sing. Bre stood up, grabbed my hand and pulled me off of my bar stool.

"Fly me to the moon," she said.

She wrapped her arms around my neck and I placed my hands upon her hips. They felt real. I inhaled. I'd not been that close to a woman in a long time and her breasts were warm and pressed against me. We danced slower than the music called for. I caught glimpses of my reflection in liquor bottles, the mirror behind the bar, foil, windows, under the neon I was pale and tinted green.

I closed my eyes, leaned in, and kissed Bre. The taste of mint still lingered on my lips when she pulled away.

"I'm married," she said. "You know that, Jackson. I'm happily married."

I had to do something. All of the waiting my life had become. Sometimes you feel yourself at a literal crossroads. It's like having a gun in your face. If you're lucky it gives you perspective and it clears a path for you. It shows you where you went wrong, and how to get the hell out of the way of it. I tried to move.

Bre backed away from me, hands up, as if she might literally need to fend me off.

"I'm okay," I said. "I just need a dollar for the jukebox. I want to play a song."

"Ruby's almost done," she said.

"Fuck Ruby. I need a goddamned dollar for the jukebox." I ran my fingers through my hair. It was greasy and lately had been falling out in bunches. It's just stress, I told myself, just stress.

"Can I have drink at least?" I asked. "I'm okay."

"No. You're not okay, Jackson. Think about it."

"Can I have a cigarette?" She handed me a Newport. I lit it. The menthol was sweet. I was on the verge. I had to tell Bre that I still loved her whether she wanted to hear it or not. Whether she could hear it over her own life, and then Ruby kicked open the green door. It banged against the wall like a gun shot. She was smiling. It was getting dark already.

"This was a night from hell," she said. "I'll have a beer before I go. Get Jackson one too. I owe him for cleaning that shelf."

Bre looked from Ruby to me and nodded. We sat at the bar.

"I drink the same thing Jackson drinks," Ruby said.

"Why tonight?" I asked. She never drank.

"It's my anniversary," she said. She drained half her beer in one swallow.

"I didn't even know you were married."

Bre grabbed my wrist from behind the bar and squeezed it gently.

"I'm not," Ruby said. "My husband shot himself after killing my daughter in a drunk driving accident. He had picked her up from church. That was...let's see, not long ago."

"Fuck," I said. "What sort of anniversary is that?" Bre squeezed my wrist even harder, like she was trying to pull me out of a nose dive.

"What kind do you think," Ruby said. "I usually did the driving. But he'd said he had somewhere to go that morning anyway. I don't know where. There were no bars open that early. I figured it would be okay."

We sat there like that. Ruby stared at me and I stared at her. Bre gripped my wrist.

"My husband was a no good rat," Ruby said. Bre closed her eyes. I took the last drink of my beer. Ruby and I sat there, our elbows propped on the bar and our hands around our beers.

"This place is a fucking mess, Ruby." I said. "You always leave this place a fucking mess."

Ruby shrugged. "You want another beer, Jackson?"

"You're a fat fucking pig, Ruby."

"You cheat on your wife," she said. "What does it matter? I'm a fat fucking pig. You drink with whores. It don't mean anything anymore. Have your drink."

"She took him back," Bre said, still gripping my wrist.

"So? What does it matter? It don't matter. You want another beer, Jackson?"

"No," I said. "I want to know why you always leave this place such a goddamned mess. I want to know why Charlie is still here. I want to know why he's always here. I want to know why he wears that stupid jacket."

"Killed our daughter," Ruby said. "Shot himself square between the eyes. Slit both his wrists first. He didn't leave anything to chance, Jackson. Not a thing."

Bre pulled at my wrist again.

"I didn't do that," I said.

"Nobody said you did." Ruby looked like a little fat imp and motioned to Bre for another beer. Bre didn't move. With my free hand, I slammed the bottom of my empty bottle onto the bar. It exploded into amber shards and cut my hand to shit.

"I don't know why you're looking at me like that," I said.

"No body said you did anything, Jackson. Cut yourself up pretty good it looks like."

"I didn't," I said. "That was your fucking husband."

Bre let go of me and I settled back onto my stool. She brought Ruby a beer. I couldn't breathe. My hand was bleeding. Ruby dug into the front pocket of her jeans. When she pulled her hand out, she was holding hundreds of four leaf clovers. She spread them across the front of the bar. She dug her hand into her pocket again and brought out more. All of them four leaf. She laid them on the bar.

"I have a lot of them," she said.

Bre dug around the drawer underneath the cash register until she found a roll of scotch tape. She handed it to me.

"Sorry," she said. "Get to work."

Ruby stood up. "I'll see you in the morning, Jackson." The green door swung on its hinges, squeaking.

Daniel Crocker's work has appeared in *The Los Angeles Review, Hobart, Big Muddy, New World Writing, Stirring, Juked, The Chiron Review, The Mas Tequila Review* and over 100 others. His books include *Like a Fish* (full length) and *The One Where I Ruin Your Childhood* (e-chap with thousands of downloads) both from Sundress Publications. Green Bean Press published several of his books in the '90s and early 2000s. These include *People Everyday and Other Poems, Long Live the 2 of Spades,* the novel *The Cornstalk Man* and the short story collection *Do Not Look Directly Into Me.* He has also published several chapbooks through various presses. His full length collection of poetry, *Shit House Rat,* was published by Spartan Press in September of 2017. Stubborn Mule Press published *Leadwood: New and Selected Poems—1998-2018* in October 2018. He was the first winner of the Gerald Locklin Prize in poetry. He is the editor of *The Cape Rock* (Southeast Missouri State University) and the co-editor of *Trailer Park Quarterly.* He's also the host of the podcast, *Sanesplaining,* about poetry, mental illness and nerd stuff. This summer, his first fiction collection, *Grown Ass Men,* in almost twenty years.